SARINA DAHLAN

# Shadow Play: Ten Tales from the In-between

*First published by The 3 Hapas in 2018*

*Copyright © Sarina Dahlan, 2018*

*This novel is entirely a work of fiction. The names, characters and incidents portrayed in it are the work of the author's imagination. Any resemblance to actual persons, living or dead, events or localities is entirely coincidental.*

*First edition*

*ISBN: 978-1-7329140-2-5*

*Cover art by Shannon Haynes*
*Editing by Nicole Lyles*
*Editing by David Dann*

*This book was professionally typeset on Reedsy.*
*Find out more at reedsy.com*

*To my husband who read every word and iteration of every story I've ever written. Without him this book would not exist.*


*To my children. For you, I write stories that I hope will contribute to a kinder, more empathetic world.*

# Contents

*Preface*                               ii
*Acknowledgement*                       iii
Shadow Play                             1
Glimmer Glass                           13
The Witch Doctor                        27
Call me Blue                            50
Love me, Tender                         61
Ghost Moon                              89
Dust Bound                              102
The Woman in the Garden                 113
The Bench                               126
Jasmine Water                           146
Afterword                               158

# Preface

I wrote this collection of stories in the space of time I have come to refer to as the "in-between." We all know this place. The gap year between high school and college or college and the real world. The months after a baby's birth. The period between jobs. The mourning time after a divorce or the death of a loved one. It is a soul-searching journey—an exploration of life's purpose and ultimate acceptance of the new.

While my inspirations for the tales can be found in the *Afterword*, my need to write them came from the desire to give voice to the in-between—that space betwixt reality and the fantastical. Here is where many things are discovered: a sense of self, the toughness of conviction, the vast landscape of the mind. It is here, in its cool dark shadow, the characters of this collection blossomed.

Sarina Dahlan
  Fall, 2018

# Acknowledgement

When I immigrated from Thailand to the U.S. at the age of twelve, I didn't know English beyond the alphabet and a few words. But my love affair with books that started when I was a child never disappeared. I dreamt of becoming a writer. It was a long road and I'll always be grateful to the following for their help along the way:

To **Dave** who suffered through my earliest (and most horrific) drafts yet continues to be my staunchest supporter. Thank you for giving me the breathing room to create and the hugs needed on those rough days I didn't fully believe in myself.

To **Shannon**, a creative genius who not only designed the beautiful cover for SHADOW PLAY, but also lent an editorial eye to my stories and typeset the hardcover version. She elevated this collection to something I am proud to call mine.

To **Nicole** who, despite having to raise a busy family, raised her hand to help beta read, offered constructive feedback, and edited the stories. With the discerning eye of an avid reader, she held me to a high standard and was honest when the stories needed to be better.

To **Simeen**, my writer friend on the other side of the world, for reading my stories. Her feedback helped me become a more thoughtful writer.

To **Jane** who never tires of cheering me on. Thank you.

To my two grandmothers, **Renoo** and **Yupa**, the yin and yang that shaped my childhood.

Also, I want to thank all my family and friends who shared with me their life stories—good and bad, funny and tragic, fantastical and real. Without you, my world would be a lot less interesting and fabulous. You gave me the inspiration to write.

Finally, I want to acknowledge the places that helped form my viewpoint. From **Kampong Java**, a little Indonesian enclave in the middle of Bangkok where I spent my first twelve years, to **California**, the state I call home. In my mind, they exist adjacent each other, sometimes blending like a perfect medley. In this collection of stories, I hope my love for these places came through.

# Shadow Play

Bangkok, Thailand, 1942

T he smell of incense tickled my nose.

It was twilight—the time of the *Jinn*. My grandmother hated that time of day. Each nightfall *Nyai* lit incense to chase away the evil spirits. It was her way of guarding her soul and mine.

The rhythmic beating of an animal skin drum came from the direction of the neighborhood mosque. Soon after, the rich melody of the *azaan*, the Muslim call to prayer from Masjid Java punctured the air. It's *Maghrib*.

*Nyai* towered above me, a lantern in her hand. The night drew harsh lines on her face, making her look like a puppet in a shadow play.

A word began to form at her mouth. *Sofia*. It was the name my mother gave me with her last breath. Sometimes I wondered whether it was what she said. It could have been something else, like Safa or Safwa, or Safia. Any Arabic name. A dying woman's last word.

*Nyai* rarely spoke of my mother, her only child. It was as though she existed just to give me life. Nyai was not a woman of many words, especially regarding the dead. We're not supposed to talk about them.

I got up from the floor and stretched. "Cold tonight."

Nyai drew her shawl tighter around her shoulders. The spot between her eyebrows folded like a fan. She did not look at me. She never looked at me squarely in the eyes since sometime after I turned thirteen. I did not know why. Maybe because I was beginning to resemble my mother. It's bad luck for a girl to look like her mom.

I wished I was more like my father. That way I would know what he looked like. Sometimes I searched for his face in those of the men I came across. Around the neighborhood. In the market. In the films they showed outdoors.

I looked for my mother's face in Nyai's sometimes. Her thin face bore traces of a once celebrated beauty. People told me that at the age of sixteen she had three neighborhood men vying for her hand in marriage. She did not end up with any of them. Instead, she chose my grandfather, an outsider.

The beauty of her youth was gone. Years of exposure to the harsh sun made her skin leathery. Four well-defined lines were etched like deep scars between her dark eyebrows. She had a wasted face—cracked like parched earth. I wondered sometimes if she thought her life was wasted. All the potential and not much to show for it except for the scrawny girl of thirteen in her care.

We performed our ablution before prayer alongside each other without words. I poured the frigid water over each of my hands.

*One, two, three.*

I brought a handful to my face.

*One, two, three.*

Nyai's movements mirrored mine. I glanced at her from the corner of my eye. I would have given anything to be able to read her mind. But she was an impenetrable rock wall. Solid. Never changing.

We walked in silence toward the prayer room. Nyai's steps were small, like those of a toddler afraid of falling. It was a strange sight because she was an unusually tall woman—almost the same height as most men. Old age made her back bend. She gave the effect of a sunflower past its prime. Wilted. Dying.

The lantern in her hand cast odd shapes that shifted and changed on the walls. I was careful to not look too long at the shadows. Evil lurked in the dark, Nyai said.

The large plank floor creaked beneath our feet. I breathed in the same rhythm as the hundred-year-old teak house, probably ever since I sucked in my first gulp of air. It was constantly moving, restless, like me.

The small prayer room sat next to Nyai's bedroom. On the floor was a threadbare rug with elaborate patterns of vines and flowers. One photograph hung on a wall—the only photograph in the house. It was a black and white image of a striking man in a light colored suit taken at a proper studio. My grandfather.

He died when my mother was a child. I did not know how or why. Just that he was still young. Too young. But what's an appropriate age to die? Seventy? Eighty?

Most everyone in my family died young. Except for Nyai. I did not know her age. She could just as well be as ancient as the house.

Our dilapidated home was the oldest and biggest in the neighborhood. Kids did not like walking by it. Sometimes I could hear them from the second story window of my bedroom telling each other fictional tales of their encounters with the spirits here. I did not blame them. If I did not live here, I would have thought the same. Our house looked haunted. Most of the rooms had been shuttered for years, abandoned to the spiders. Furniture draped in dusty sheets. Forts of mildewed boxes. Moth-eaten curtains. Relics of Nyai's past. It was not always this way.

The house was built for children, many of them. Over the decades, as the children grew, sections were added to accommodate multiple families and generations. At one point there were over twenty souls under one roof. Sometimes I imagined this house filled with the sounds of life—kids screeching, chasing one another; a father bringing in wood for burning; wives making dinner in the kitchen. The house remembered those sounds too and would mimic them as it settled and creaked.

The handsome dead man in a fancy sterling silver frame stared at me with smiling eyes. He looked as if he had a secret he wanted to tell but could not. I did not know much about him. Nyai did not speak of

3

him either, but the echo of my grandfather's presence was everywhere in our house. His books. His furniture. His paintings.

In our white *telekung* we prayed. Nyai stood in front of me and recited my favorite verse from the Qu'ran as she did every *Maghrib* prayer:

*Qul a'uudhu bi rabbin naas*
Say, "I seek refuge with the Lord and Cherisher of Mankind,"
*Malikin naas*
The King of Mankind,
*Ilaahin naas*
The God of Mankind,
*Min sharri waswaasii khannas*
From the evil of the retreating whisperer,
*Alladhee yawaswisu fee suduurin naas*
Who whispers into the hearts of Mankind,
*Minal Jinnati wa naas*
From among Jinns and among men.

Nyai said this *surat* to keep the evil spirits at bay. My grandmother and I, we were surrounded by ghosts. *Kampong Java* was a perfect site for that. Four cemeteries hemmed in our Javanese neighborhood in the heart of Bangkok, forming an imperfect rhombus.

The biggest of the four was a Chinese burial ground. It had elaborate stone crypts and a multi-storied pagoda with bright red roofs. Next to it was a *wat*, a Buddhist temple where monks chanted in the ancient language of Pali to send off the departed. The *wat* had a tall incinerator used for burning bodies.

The farthest cemetery, about a fifteen-minute walk away, was the oldest Catholic churchyard in Bangkok. The orange brick church had a high pitched roof modeled after the roof line on a traditional Thai house. It had a bell in the tall white tower. I never saw the bell but I heard it many times, so I knew it was there.

The closest to my house was the Muslim cemetery—what everyone in my neighborhood called a *kubor*. Many hair-raising ghost stories came out of this section of Bangkok. This was not a place you walked alone after dark.

We finished the prayer and Nyai began her *duah*, a request to God. I watched her get lost in that one-sided conversation and wondered what she asked for. She could sit there for hours.

She had a tendency to disappear in her own silence. When she got that way, I would picture her walking around in a maze inside her head, hitting dead ends and turning around many times before finding her way out.

A knock on the door and my heart jolted against the bones of my chest. I looked at Nyai but she was still absorbed in her *duah* and dialogue with God.

"Who could that be?" I asked.

She said nothing back.

*Maybe the neighbor needed something.* I got up. Blood rushed back into my legs, sending pinpricks of pain through them like ants biting my skin with their pinchers.

I trekked toward the front of the house past a row of paintings so real they looked almost like photographs. A vast expanse of a green forest; bright blue ocean with a cloudless sky; temples with faces etched in stones; a bare-chested dancer with red flowers on her crown. My prayer outfit billowed in the breeze that snuck in through the gaps between the shiplap walls, sending chills up my legs.

The heavy teak front door stood formidably like a dark gate to the netherworld. I unbolted the iron lock and yanked it with all my strength. The door swelled after the rain, which happened as often as not.

There was no one there. The only living thing was a skinny cat patrolling the garden. He saw me and darted away.

The bright colors on the step below caught my attention. Flowers. White, red, yellow, and blue. They sat like passengers stuffed tightly inside a small boat-shaped basket made of palm leaf. I squatted to pick it up. The sweet scent of roses and jasmine touched my nose. I prodded the garland with my finger, finding pleasure in the velvety softness of the petals. A feeling of peace, anesthetizing and warm, draped over me like a blanket.

Strange rumblings like distant thunder startled me out of my stupor. At a distance, in the direction of the Chao Phraya river, spots of bright orange lit up the sky.

*Fireworks?*

I gathered the skirt of my *telekung* above my knees so it would not touch the mud puddle from the last rain and stepped into my sandals. Outside, the air was crisp and I could see my breath in white puffs. The moon hung round like a lantern on the deep indigo sky. A few wispy clouds floated along like ghost ships on a vast ocean.

It could not be fireworks. The First of January was last week. The Japanese had control of the city and there was no celebration.

A series of sharp blasts perforated the night and a half ball of light lit up the horizon. The ground purred beneath my feet. The brightness died down, replaced by a band the color of sunset. Red and orange flames slithered up the sky like sinuated snakes. The Chao Phraya was on fire.

My heart thumped violently inside the cavity of my chest. I began to suck in gulps of air. The sound of someone else's scream and my beating heart competed against each other in my ears. A hundred thoughts raced around in my head, trying to be the first to get my attention. The loudest won out.

*This is it. This is when we die.*

I recited my favorite surat. The orange spots in the sky faded. The rumbling ceased. My breathing began to slow.

Suddenly a different sound—thunderous like a fast-approaching violent storm. The deafening roar grew until it overwhelmed everything. I looked up and saw several groups of small planes flying overhead. No matter how hard I tried, I could not take my eyes off them. I was exposed like a rabbit frozen by the sight of a hawk above.

For a moment I thought I was standing underneath a lightning strike.

The brightness hurt my eyes. It was like staring into the sun. Then just as fast, the planes disappeared, taking the sound with them until it was but a memory of a bad dream.

My grandmother's face came to me, jolting me back. A wave of goosebumps travelled down the planes of my body. I ran inside and slammed the heavy door against the frame.

Nyai was still sitting on the spot I left her in the prayer room. She was no longer wearing her *telekung*. Her disheveled white hair draped like silk threads over one shoulder. She looked wild, like an ancient creature one could find in a primordial forest. Her eyes were wide with fear. In them, an overflowing winter river.

*What do I tell her?*

"I saw planes flying above our house. They came from the direction of the river. There were orange lights in the sky," I said it in a tone I imagined a brave person would use.

She said nothing back. Her hands were stroking her chest. She was trying to stay calm too.

"It's over though. It's quiet again," I said and sat down across from her.

I looked down at my lap and noticed my left hand was not empty. In it was the small basket of flowers. I had forgotten about it.

"I found this on the front step," I told her as I massaged the soft petals. "I don't know who left it."

Outside, the morning had evolved into a busy day. From my second-story bedroom window, I could hear for kilometers—fruit and vegetable sellers paddling boats up the stream to the market, the dinging of the trolley bells on the main street, the shouting of the Chinese man who went door-to-door offering knife sharpening service. But the most prominent sound that came through my window, what woke me up each morning, was the Muslim call to prayer from the mosque.

Nyai told me we were lucky to be living so close to the masjid. It was the center of life in our neighborhood. Everything happened there: babies' head shaving ceremonies, animal sacrifices, Qur'an graduations, circumcisions, funeral prayers. The place was constantly humming with people. We lived and died by the mosque.

In a distance, I saw a plume of white smoke spewing out of the tall incinerator at the Buddhist temple. There were deaths last night—people killed by the bombs dropped from the British and American planes. The *farang* were warring with the Japanese, the Japanese were in Thailand, and so they were warring with us. Everything had changed. The war was no longer something that happened thousands of kilometers away in the lands of snow-capped mountains.

Buddhists believed in reincarnation. After death, they would return to this earth as another form of life, depending on the karma they had accumulated. The good ones moved up in status until they reached nirvana. The horrible ones came back as a *Pred*, a ghost as tall as a coconut tree with a mouth as small as a pinhole. They wandered cemeteries in the middle of the night, moaning from a painful hunger that could not be tamed.

Nyai told me none of it was true. She had her own version of life after death that sounded just as gruesome. I preferred to think the deceased rose up into the sky and became rain clouds.

The day spread out like a prayer rug in front of me. There was no school today. There had been no school since the Japanese occupied the city. People moved out in droves to their relatives in the country. Nyai and I had no one so we were stuck in our dilapidated house in the flight path of bombers.

I navigated the garden in sandals that splattered wet dirt onto my calves as I walked. Nyai did not allow me to leave the grounds of the house. There were rumors of young women raped by Japanese soldiers and left for dead. Even though my body, flat chest and straight hips, still resembled a child's, my grandmother did not want the worry.

I wished for my mother. I missed her—or whatever feeling one could have for someone they have no memories of. Against Nyai's order, I

8

decided to let my feet carry me past the masjid and across the street. *Just for a little bit.*

Through a creaky green gate with a crescent moon and star, I entered the kubor. The temperature was cooler here. Several mature trees dominated the ground. Large jade green leaves spread like umbrellas over the rich black dirt beneath. A small white gazebo stood lonely in the middle of the cemetery.

The dewy smell of wet earth commingled with the sweet scent of jasmine permeated the air. I breathed in a lung full of the floral bouquet. Flowering plants of various colors were scattered around different types of tomb markers. White, red, yellow, and blue. Some markers were simple wooden stakes. The names on some were faded from age. Some did not even have a name. I walked toward the area where my mother and grandfather were buried.

In mid-step, a fear overcame me—irrational and palpable. It felt eerily similar to last night when every bone in my body rooted me in place as the planes flew overhead. I thought of Nyai, turned and ran.

I did not stop until I reached the gate of the house. After I crossed it, my eyes caught sight of a familiar object sitting on the ground at one corner of the house. I walked closer to it and recognized the small basket of colorful flowers. I picked it up. The tiny boat of woven palm leaves looked to be made by the same hands as the one I found last night. Except this time there was a tiny lump of palm sugar, hardened into the shape of a *chedi*, a stupa on temple ground.

Sugar was hard to come by in the time of war. *Why would anyone leave it on the ground as if it had no value?* I looked side to side and over my shoulder. No one was around. I picked up the candy and dropped it on my tongue. The nugget melted, setting an explosion of intense sweetness inside my mouth. For a moment I was reminded of a time before—of friends, school, and life outside the house.

I continued strolling. At a different corner of the house, I found another basket of flowers with a lump of palm sugar. By the time I made one loop around the building, I had eaten four nuggets. My spirit was high when I reached the front door.

On the steps I saw a pair of woman's shoes. A guest! Nobody visited us anymore. I shook off my sandals and splashed some water from a small earthen pot just outside the door threshold onto my mud-stained feet. The freezing water made the hair on my arms and legs stand up. I forced open the stubborn door and entered.

The house was quiet. Having remembered my grandmother received visitors in the formal living room, I walked toward it. It was the richest room in our worn house. In it were western-style sofas the color of pink lotus and matching chintz curtains. Between the sofas was a large round wood table, polished to a gleam. A pair of silver candleholders stood proudly on it.

I heard whispering coming from the room connected to the living room—my grandmother's bedroom. I walked toward the sound and looked through the gap of the door. My grandmother was sitting on the bed with her back to me. In front of her was a woman.

"Hello," I said and pushed the door open.

The woman smiled. "Sofia. You're here."

It was Pa Mali, Nyai's friend and the local witch doctor. She lived across the street from the *kubor*—ironic for the only non-Muslim in our neighborhood. If a house could look more haunted than ours, it was hers. It sat far back from the road, half hidden by several mature mango trees and overgrown shrubberies. It stood high above ground on four stilts and had a high pitched roof with ends that curved up like a man's mustache. It was the only traditional Thai home left in the neighborhood.

She had many gifts, but the one most often used was her doctoring. I had been to her a few times for magic bananas to ease stomach pain and herbs for headaches. Many went to her for all types of ailments. It cost too much to go to the hospital. Almost nobody I knew went to the hospital unless they were dying. Sometimes not even then.

A feeling of doom descended—sticky and bitter like tree sap.

"Is she okay?" I asked, my voice trembling. She had to be. Nyai was the only family I had left.

My grandmother's back was still turned to me. She was silent as if made of stone.

"She will be," Pa Mali said.

"What's wrong with her?"

"She's grieving."

I did not blame her. Nyai's life was one intimate with loss. She had to bury her husband and daughter sooner than anyone should have to.

"I went to their graves today—my mom's and grandpa's," I said and remembered the rule. "Well, I turned back before I got there. I'm not supposed to be away from the house."

I looked at my grandmother's back. Melancholy leached off her. It thickened the air, making it hard to breathe.

"I never knew them," I said. *Could one properly grieve someone without knowing them?*

"You haven't seen them?" Pa Mali asked.

"I've never met them."

It was odd she asked me that question. She was the one who delivered me bloodied and slicked from my mother's womb and watched her die afterward. The thought was quickly eclipsed by an abrupt intense desire to know my mom.

"What was my mother like?"

"Beautiful with long hair that blanketed her entire back. She was very smart. The first girl in the Kampong to have gone to a university."

My grandmother's back shook from the force of her sob. I knew I should stop my questioning. Nyai did not like talking about the dead.

"I want to go to a university," I said wistfully. Once the war was over. Once schools opened again.

Pa Mali's eyes welled up. She was not one accustomed to crying. I looked at her, perplexed by her emotion.

"What's wrong?" I asked.

She did not answer. Instead, her eyes were focused on the stack of flower baskets in my hand.

"It's the weirdest thing. I keep finding these on the ground all around the house," I said.

"They're spirit offerings. The flowers all have meanings. Jasmine for purity. Roses for spiritual joy. Marigolds for auspiciousness. Blue lotus for wisdom—like your name."

White, red, yellow, blue.

"But ghosts are dead," I said.

"The spirit world perceives differently than the physical world, but that doesn't mean they can't experience things in ways the human mind remembers."

"So they like flowers?"

"It can be anything. Burning incense, candles, food. It's a way to honor the memory of the deceased."

My face warmed.

"I ate the candies that were on the offerings," I confessed.

"It's okay. They were for you."

The space between my eyebrows folded together like the way my grandmother's did when she looked in my direction. "You left them? For me? Why?"

"Your grandmother wanted me to."

*Why would Nyai do that?* I looked at her back. The wordless woman continued to ignore my existence. I walked toward her and placed my palm on her shoulder, intending to make her turn to acknowledge me. But my hand could never quite reach her. Her body was in front of me yet it felt far away.

I looked at my hands. The flowers were gone. *Where did they go?* These hands—this body—felt as if they belonged to a stranger. My head throbbed to the beat of my heart. *Thm. Thm. Thm. Thm.*

"Something's wrong," I said, my voice trembling.

"Tell her I miss her," Nyai said.

*The war had changed everything.*

# Glimmer Glass

Cooperstown, U.S.A., 2001

The crisp morning was as picture-perfect as could be. Henry looked at the glittering lake out the windows of the dark cabin that was his for the month. Its surface was a calm blue, reflecting the summer sky where there was not a single cloud. Lake Otsego, the source of the Susquehanna River, featured prominently in his mind, coloring every single act in his life, even one as mundane as urinating. It was a thing he liked to do in the lake as a kid. As he did, he would imagine a part of him flowing through decayed towns and thriving cities to the Chesapeake Bay, before draining into the Atlantic. The water was now too cold for his septuagenarian bones.

On the other side of the lake, a mile away, he could see rolling emerald hills and peek-a-boo cottages nestled between trees. A boat with a bright white sail drifted by like a toy in a bathtub. This place, this town, was his best memory of childhood encapsulated—petrified like the fossils he hunted when he was a boy. It never strayed far from his mind, regardless of how many countries he had travelled to in his life as a journalist.

The cabin was once the old summer camp's administration office, where as a camper he only stepped inside a handful of times. In all the years after it dissolved and transformed, it seemed the owner had done nothing to it except change the furniture and put down carpet. The familiar smell was still there—musky and earthy, like waterlogged forest floor. This scent was not limited to the inside of the cabin but everywhere, as if it was the essence of the color green itself.

The owner, a member of a prominent Cooperstown family, had inherited it from a great-aunt who had inherited it from her father. Since the current owner was born too late to have known it as a boys' camp, he had decided to use it as a summer rental. It was not outfitted for the long winters, as it had no insulation nor central heat. Nor air conditioning for that matter. Sometimes, when it was windy, Henry could feel a draft coming in through the ill-fitted windows and doors. But it suited him just fine. He was used to the changing temperament of weather.

He took a sip of the mint tea. His stomach had been bothering him lately. At his age, food had become his enemy. He loved it still, but it was a one-sided relationship. There was no one to blame but himself, having lived his life as if he did not have an expiration date, punishing his body with work, drinks, drugs, and the unhealthiest food he could find. The problem was that his genetics were too good. Tall and slim, he looked as fit as if he had exercised regularly. If he had looked the way he felt, the signs would have been more obvious.

The drugs were in the past, as was work. He even learned to cook for himself since the nearest restaurant was twenty minutes away in the downtown area near the Baseball Hall of Fame. He still drank. It was the only way he could sleep. But for now he was content with the mint tea.

He opened the desk drawer and pulled out a journal. Black-bound with snow-white pages. He intended to fill it with the messiness of the life he had lived. But he could not decide where to begin. The beginning is everything. Done wrong and it would taint the entire story.

He could start with his childhood at the camp, swimming in the refreshing water and sneaking cigarettes in the shade of the trees. He could talk about stealing away after everyone had gone to bed to sail across the lake to his sweetheart's home just to get a glimpse of her through lit windows. Or the time his boat ran aground on Sunken Island, a submerged sandy plot near the western shore, where he spent the night being eaten alive by mosquitos.

Under the green shade of oaks and hemlocks, he took his time growing up. It was an era when adults were not fearful and kids were allowed to explore. Here was where he learned to shoot with target rifles, sail, and fall in love. On second thought, all those moments seemed too precious. His life was the opposite of precious.

Maybe he could talk about his work as a war correspondent. The darkness and pain he encountered in the lives of those who had everything yanked out of their hands. The sunken, glazed look in children's eyes as they tried to make sense of the chaos surrounding them by constructing a new way of seeing in a world where death and life were separated by a hairbreadth and a wrong turn. The heartbreaking image of a soldier who, in the previous moment killed his enemies without mercy, was embracing the corpse of his dead friend with the tenderness of a father to his son. But how could Henry explain everything he had seen in words? The complexity of humanity in the field of war was not something easily captured. Even the pictures and the videos lacked the depth of feelings embedded inside each moment. Its reality was lost to those who have always lived in peace. One must be there to know it and to hate it in order to understand it.

He had dedicated his entire life to telling stories no one wanted to tell or hear. But he could say that, in a way, his old profession took part in perpetuating the existence of war. Hearing it in words and seeing its images only put a veil around it, marking it as something that happened to other people and in places far away. Those stories he wrote—black words on white paper surrounded by borders—only dug trenches around the atrocity, separating it from daily life, drawing a line between 'them' and 'us'.

A familiar melancholy descended. He felt his shoulders hunching as if a blanket of metal chains had been placed upon him. He pulled it with both hands and wrapped it tight around his body, letting it become one with his skin. This heaviness was the only constant thing in his life, trailing him like a caravan of spirits.

Outside, Lake Otsego and the sky were still blue. But so was his mood. He looked at the mint tea that was still emitting white steam and knew it was not enough. He opened another drawer and pulled out a bottle of Redbreast whiskey. Irish. Twelve-year-old cask-strength. It was still too early—oh well. He poured it into a shot glass he always kept next to the bottle. Once half-filled, he picked it up and drained it into his mouth with one flick of his wrist. The warmth travelled down his throat into the void inside, coating it with hints of honeyed sweetness and peppery notes.

He wanted to pour another but did not. Instead he closed his eyes and started the process. It was a ritual he had been following since the day a friend who suffered the same affliction taught it to him. He began counting.

*One.* He was born. With each number he was supposed to think of the images associated with that year. He did not always remember everything of course. Those that he did not remember he would make up the details like a fictional novel or leave blank like overexposed film. This image—a journey through a red tunnel that ended with the warmth of his mother's embrace—was one inspired by a documentary on the Science channel.

*Two.* Walking. He learned the freedom that came with it. He fell often. *Four.* Books. He discovered reading. With that, endless endings in an endless number of worlds opened up to him.

*Eight.*

*Eight.*

The images were blurry, but he forced himself to look at them, climbing their thorny trunks as if he were self-flagellating. It was important to the ritual that he embrace the pain, his friend told him. Count. See. Embrace. That was the process.

*Eight was Mother.* That year, she died. It was a short illness. The last time he saw her she was lying on a bed with her curly hair spraying behind her. She was wearing a beautiful lace nightgown his father had purchased from New York City. She looked like a princess from a fairytale, sleeping, waiting for her one true love to kiss her. But no matter the number of kisses, she never awoke.

His dad was a busy executive who travelled often. Henry was an only child. Add a dead mother and it was a perfect recipe for lost souls. His father decided he could not handle both running a company in the middle of the Depression and a grieving child at the same time, so he sent Henry to a private boarding school during the school year and a camp during the summer. And so this place became a refuge from his parents' absence.

*Nine. Ten. Eleven. Twelve.* The images were of the lake and the camp. This nook of land next to the lake was an idyllic place for a boy to discover himself. Rudimentary and simple, everything at the camp, aside from eating, was done outdoors. He slept in an old-fashioned canvas tent on a raised wooden platform. He took soap baths in the lake. He urinated (when not in the lake) into funnels placed in strategic spots along the tent line. For heavier duty bodily functions, he used the "Palace", a room of toilets (thrones) sitting next to each other with no dividers in between.

At the lake, he learned the concept of responsibility. If he did not bathe, he would stay dirty. If he did not eat at a designated time, he would go hungry. He bonded with other boys while hiking through ravines and listening to campfire ghost stories, not over the professions of their fathers nor the size of their mansions as was the custom at his boarding school.

*Seventeen.* Sweet seventeen. The image that came to him was of a girl from across the lake with whom he fell in love with for the first time. She was beautiful, blonde and vivacious with a smile that melted his heart. When he kissed her the world became bright and full of possibilities. The first time they made love, he imagined a life with her in Cooperstown, farming the land and growing old next to her. But like many young romances, it did not last past a summer.

*Eighteen.* He saw leather bound books and red brick buildings with towers and turrets. He was at an Ivy League college—his dad's alma mater—that promised a successful life inside the luxury of wealth. *Nineteen.* He left college to join the Air Force, wanting to avenge the death of his countrymen who perished at Pearl Harbor. *Twenty.* He flew across the globe for the war in the Pacific, bombing cities where the enemy resided. He saw in shades of orange and red—the colors he had come to associate with destruction. He did not know how many he had killed. He did not want to know. It was easy to do it from a bird's eye view. Honorable, even. He was doing good by fighting evil, he told himself.

In this period of his life, he learned that war has a habit of taking everything precious from everyone it touches. With every bloom of explosion he caused below and every shot he sustained from the enemy, his sense of optimism, his love of life, and his sanity was whittled away. It was not until 1980 that the American Psychiatric Association added Post Traumatic Stress Disorder to the third edition of its Diagnostic and Statistical Manual of Mental Disorders. Before then he did not know the affliction he suffered from for decades had a name.

*Twenty-three.* He came back to the same college, but everything had changed. He no longer felt a part of that world and its frivolity. He changed his major to English to the disapproval of his father. He grew a beard and learned to love again. But love was also different and each woman left because they could never own him. He was not there.

After graduation, everyone he knew got married and had children. At times he felt the pressure of expectation, yet he could never bring himself to cross the threshold. It was as if he was standing outside his life, watching it as if it did not belong to him.

*Twenty-six.* He left with one suitcase to New York City and began working at a newspaper. It was there he developed a love for strong black coffee and undiluted whiskey. By then he was so far off the life track his father had planned for him that they stopped speaking. It happened so gradually that Henry did not feel a great sense of loss.

They had nothing in common except for the holes left in their lives by the woman they both loved. Since neither wanted to talk about her, there was nothing for them to discuss.

His New York years were a chaotic box of black and white photographs taken as he walked its streets. Men in long trench coats and fedoras buying tickets at Grand Central Station. An army of pigeons under Time Square's movie advertisement signs. Young women in smart skirt suits, high heels off, sitting in front of a secretarial school between classes. Park benches and fallen maple leaves in Central Park. Sometime during those years, the call to join the Korean War came. He declined. It had been too soon.

By 1955, he was thirty-three and restless. A war in Vietnam had just started. In the decade after World War II, Southeast Asia had undergone revolutionary changes, having released itself from the grip of colonialism. Communism was taking root and Henry was again drawn to the region. He convinced his editor to send him to Asia and established himself as the journalist there, long before the American troops were deployed to Vietnam in 1965.

For him, Southeast Asia was less an image than a feeling. Warm and sinuous, it curled around him like a cat. At times it sat quietly on his lap, letting him explore its soft fur and mesmerizing feline features. At other times, when its wildness returned, it would leave him scarred.

In his forties he fell head-over-heels in love. This time with another war journalist. She looked like Brigitte Bardot, but her vocabulary could put a sailor to shame. An untamable spirit, she was powerful and relentless in her pursuit of honesty. With her he felt brave and unstoppable, as if together they could topple governments and change the course of the world. Simply with words. It was an intense and all-consuming love affair.

Henry opened his eyes. He poured another shot of whiskey. Down the hatch. The warmth glazed his empty stomach like icing. The top of his lips began to feel numb. Anger arose. He capped the whiskey and shoved it back into the abyss of the desk drawer. He picked up the cup of tea, which was now lukewarm, and drank the whole thing.

Henry closed his eyes again and saw only his lover's face. She died in Vietnam. Not by bullets nor bombs, but from a disease she contracted. The two years after was a blank. As Vietnam struggled against itself and outside forces, he was fighting to stay alive inside the pit of darkness that was his sorrow. It swallowed him whole, drowning him in drink and tears. The only thing that saved him was the war. Under fire, his body reacted to survive. In those moments he found purity of feelings—fear, love, hate, anger—and the eventual salvation. It came in the form of a child.

She was a girl who looked to be eight, the age he was when he lost his mother. He found her amongst the rubble of the village the American jets had just bombed. He took her to a makeshift hospital in a makeshift U.S. camp and sat with her as she was being treated by a medical technician for her cuts and bruises. With his minimal Vietnamese, he learned that her entire family had just died in the bombing. In her he saw a loss so absolute, his own felt insignificant. He left her to cover another assignment with a promise to return. But when he did, she was no longer there. Neither was the makeshift camp. The Viet Cong got them all.

He finally returned to America on his fiftieth birthday. By then he had had enough of the war and the constant wetness of Southeast Asia. All he wanted was to feel dry again.

Stateside, instead of peace, he was faced with a fight more personal. His dad was ailing from the latent broken heart he had suffered decades before. By his hospital bed, Henry sat and listened to the old man talk about his dead wife and the perfect life they had together. As Henry silently acknowledged that losing the love of their life was another thing they had in common, his father left this world. It was a Friday. By Monday Henry buried him next to his mother in their hometown.

*Fifty-one.* He moved into his father's house and become a professor, teaching journalism to college kids with long hair and a penchant for wielding big words like swords to advance their truth. It was the age after Watergate and the height of idealism. To them he told stories about the young soldiers he marched with under monsoon rain and heavy humidity. It's too easy to think of the other side as sub-human, he reminded them. That was how wars got started and morality became muddled. In the end, everyone was just a pawn in the game of the rich and the powerful. A good journalist, he said, began each story with people at its core. Forget that and they may just as well write propaganda.

Henry enjoyed being a professor more than he should. There, he began an affair with a student half his age. She wanted to change the world like the rest of them. She reminded him of his lost lover. The long blonde hair. The willowy figure. The smile. Although she loved him, his feelings for her never matured past casual encounters in his bedroom. She left him after a year, because it was too difficult to compete with a ghost.

The cuckoo clock struck eight. Henry opened his eyes. Lake Otsego glistened in the morning sun, befitting its nickname, *Glimmerglass*. He was not done counting yet. There were still twenty-eight to go, but he was exhausted. The process always did that to him. The first few times he did it, the images that rushed through were so painful that he despised living even more. But the more he practiced the ritual, the clearer the reason for it became.

*Life is suffering.*

*But in it is also heartbreaking beauty.*

*Count. See. Embrace.*

*That is the process of living.*

Henry asked his friend whether that was the intention of the exercise, to which he had answered with a shrug. A few years after that his friend lost his struggle against his own demons, leaving Henry to earn each number alone.

He began to feel the anchor of sadness again. He closed his eyes and forced himself to finish counting. Where was he? *Fifty-five.* He went back to New York City and journalism. With a few awards to his name, it was not hard to restart that life. Writing was writing. It was 1977 and the city was going through a dark period. He covered stories on the Son of Sam, a serial killer who shot victims with a .44 caliber revolver and left mocking letters for the police.

Then there was the Blackout. One night in July, New York City and its vicinity were plunged into darkness from a power outage. In a city in the middle of a financial crisis and a murder spree, frustrated people took to the street, resulting in citywide looting and arson. 1977 was filled with red and orange images.

He muddled through the next decade or so, combining working and drinking with the drugging of the eighties. He only remembered the eighties for the year that mattered. 1989. He was *sixty-seven*. Henry went back to the front line once more. The U.S. invaded Panama to capture General Noriega on drug charges after he fell out of favor as a CIA asset in their war against Nicaragua. What Henry saw there were contradictory sides of the Panamanians' reaction to the American troops. While on television, the people cheered Operation Just Cause. But there were whispered curses too. Many lost family and friends in the cross-fire in the impoverished El Chorrillo neighborhood and saw soldiers hauling away dead bodies in trucks to be buried in a mass grave. The death toll was significantly more than what the mainstream media advertised. He and a few colleagues chose to tell different stories than what were sanctioned. His article was buried, and the truth with it. After seeing objective journalism standing by the wayside, he left the business for good.

After retirement, his life was a series of moments in front of the TV. *Sixty-eight.* The Hubble Space Telescope launch. *Sixty-nine.* The Persian Gulf War. He remembered watching as a journalist listed in a dispassionate voice the arsenal of the U.S.

Tomahawk cruise missiles launched toward key targets in Baghdad.

Stealth fighters, first used in Panama, took out targets in Western Iraq.

B-52s, carrying thousands of pounds of bombs (with far more

advanced technology than the B-29 he flew in the Pacific) obliterated buildings.

Wild Weasel war planes.

Apache helicopters.

F-15. F-14. A-10 Warthogs.

His country had become more efficient at killing. He remembered wondering how many more soldiers would return home with PTSD, how many more children would be without parents, and how increasingly callous the world was becoming.

His stomach growled. Eight thirty. Time for breakfast. He got up—his ritual hanging in the air like a floating speck of dust. He promised himself he would come back to it. He needed sustenance for combat.

Henry went into the kitchen. In the small fridge he found a head of broccoli, a package of chicken breast, and a carton of eggs. In the carton was a single egg—his weekly limit per his physician. But he felt like two this morning. He also felt like pancakes and a side of crispy hash browns. He definitely did not have ingredients for those.

He walked to his bedroom and changed into a pair of pants as a public service. No one should have to suffer his old man's legs. Not even he, if he had a choice.

Outside the cabin, the air was cool with a slight breeze. He stepped gingerly off the porch and onto the rickety wood stairs. Alone and at his age, he couldn't afford to fall. An image flashed—him struggling on his back like an overturned turtle, trying to get up—and he shuddered. Once his feet found the ground, a mixture of mulch and gravel, he felt better. He walked to the car, the one he had rented from the city. He did not like to drive, but out here you needed transportation.

Inside it still had the new car smell. Henry started the engine and the radio came on. He turned it off, wanting to prolong the silence. He eased his car up the long dirt road and onto the quiet two-lane that looped around the lake.

The scenery was magical. A canopy of trees cast green light on the winding road, making everything, even his skin, take on the hue. One side of the road sloped up, a forest of hemlock and hardwoods to the mountain ridge where as a kid he hiked in search of florescent mushrooms. At the bottom of it were creek beds where he found prehistoric shell and trilobite fossils. The other side of the road angled down gently toward the lake. He could see it between trees and homes, with the latter fortunately still few and far in between. A foundation run by a prominent Cooperstown family owned and maintained large parcels of land around the lake, contributing to its preservation.

Henry's car crawled into the downtown area. To his left was a green field with an Indian burial mound behind a low wall. At the base of the mound, Native American remains excavated from the field were reburied. Some of the ghost stories he heard around the campfires were inspired by this place.

The red brick Baseball Hall of Fame, first built when he was fourteen, was quiet. He had yet to set foot inside it. He did not know why. Maybe he was taking for granted the fact that it was always there and seemed would always be there. Or maybe he was the only New Yorker who did not care for baseball.

He parked in front of a restaurant that served breakfast. He went to the door and pulled. It was locked. He looked at his watch and the operating hours on the door. It should have been open. He peered inside. The lights were on but it was empty of people.

He looked around. A couple of blocks up, on the other side of the street, was a couple walking. But aside from them, the sidewalks were empty. He wondered whether it was a holiday, and he had forgotten. He could not remember today's date. His stomach growled.

He went to the restaurant next door. Closed. He tried the ice cream shop next to it. Closed. Frustrated, he went back to his car.

Inside, he remembered the ritual he had left unfinished. A small part of him—the superstitious part he gained while living a decade in Southeast Asia—wondered whether he would have to pay for this neglect somehow. But he was too hungry to bother.

He thought of the bread and pasta in the cupboard, and the broccoli and chicken in the fridge. He would eat those for breakfast. With a plan in place, he felt better.

As the car rolled past lush trees and ravines, he rolled down his window and stuck out his arm. With his left hand, he surfed the air like a dolphin through waves. Up. Down. Up. Down. It was a beautiful day.

A voice in the back of his mind reminded him to finish his counting. Only ten more to go. But the sky was too blue and the wind was too nice. Aside from the hunger pangs in his gut, he was feeling good. He could stop at sixty-nine, he told himself. Sixty-nine was a good number.

He reached over to the radio button and pushed. NPR morning edition.

*Breaking news from New York City, where planes—two planes have hit both towers of the World Trade Center in lower Manhattan. The upper floors, a hundred and ten story high, each tower... Television networks were showing pictures of the first crash which occurred shortly before nine o'clock. The second plane hit the second tower moments after, maybe five or ten minutes past nine o'clock eastern time this morning.*

*—smashed right into the building. It's incomprehensible.*

*I can see black smoke billowing from both towers. Debris is raining down onto the busy streets below.*

*Right now, what we know is that there will be enormous injuries and deaths.*

*The FBI is investigating a possible hijacking.*

*The scene is unreal. We were in the kitchen cooking. We heard a big explosion. And we saw big holes with flames. We saw people falling off the building. At least a dozen. Ten minutes later we heard another boom and saw a huge hole in the other World Trade Center.*

*We saw people jump. From high up. Like they were going to jump in a parachute.*

Henry eased his car into the parking spot at the bottom of the long driveway. He sat, keys still in the ignition, staring into Lake Otsego. His hands went to the collar of his shirt. He began to unbutton. One by one, the buttons opened. The cool air touched his chest, sending prickles down the plane of his body. He peeled off his shirt and threw it onto the passenger seat.

He opened the door and got out. He unbuckled his belt and unzipped. His pants fell onto the ground with a clink of the metal buckle. He shrugged off his sandals. The bottom of his soles felt both the softness of dead leaves and the hardness of gravel. With only his boxers between him and nature, he walked to the beach. He stepped onto the wooden boat ramp. At the end of the ramp, he eased himself in.

The water was cold. Colder than he had remembered. But it did not matter. He leaned back and found that he could still float like he used to when he was a kid. Blue sky filled his entire vision. Clear azure. Not a cloud in sight. There would be days to come for questioning and crying; for connecting the dots and laying blame; for regretting and reasoning. But not today. At least not for him.

Henry closed his eyes. This day would always be *seventy-nine* for as long as he lived. He imagined a part of his body flowing through decayed towns and thriving cities to the Chesapeake Bay before draining into the Atlantic where now floated the ashes of the dead and the missing.

*One.*

# The Witch Doctor

Bangkok, Thailand, 1942

Fah paddled her boat through the streets, passing the sunken doors of homes, naked kids swimming, and half-submerged trees. From the window of a house, a man dangled a fishing line. He settled on the sill, one leg hanging down like Buddha's earlobe. His eyes flitted between the cloudless blue sky above and the water below as if he could not decide which was at fault. Seeing him made the girl wonder whether there were fish inside her own home.

A few weeks ago her father found a large black snake on the first floor and killed it with a hatchet. The entire family had moved upstairs since. Her mother even installed a makeshift kitchen in the hallway. There was now a growing soot stain on the ceiling from the small coal stove.

The water had been slow to recede. It covered the first story of her house to her calves, seeping into the fiber of every piece of furniture too heavy and bulky to move, destroying it from the inside. She felt sorry for the teak cabinets each time she waded past. They stood like shipwrecks, run aground on an ebbing tide. But there was nothing her family could do. They, too, were casualties of the flood.

Their entire garden was under water. The long beans, the chilis, the kaffir lime, the basil, the eggplant, and all the green-leaf vegetables disappeared as if stolen by fairies. An entire coop of chickens drowned. It was the first time she saw her mother cry. It would be nice to have a free fish for dinner. Her stomach growled.

Her boat rocked. Startled, she whipped her head to look behind her. A brave child was hanging onto the tail of her boat. He smiled, his lips stretching from ear to ear showing a missing row of front teeth. His weight made it harder to paddle but she did not have the heart to shoo him away. How could she be angry when they were suffering the same fate?

Almost everybody in her neighborhood near the river lost something. But what could they do? You cannot get mad at Mother Nature. The rain had been heavier than usual in the northeast and northwest of Thailand. The water travelled, guided by its memory, and flooded the Chao Phraya and its tributaries. Bangkok, being in the central plain on the river's path to the Gulf, was now under meters of water. Many buildings and homes were destroyed, as were rice fields and groves. It was no one's fault.

In its own way, the flood also made the city strangely beautiful. Surrounded by glittering tea-colored water and cleansed of soot and dust, it looked otherworldly. At least through the eyes of a fifteen-year-old.

There were other unexpected blessings as well. Since the streets were not walkable, the Japanese soldiers took to staying inside their bases instead of patrolling. The Allies, in turn, were dropping fewer bombs from their attack planes, not wanting to waste them. The flood gave everyone respite from the relentlessness of war.

The boy let go of her boat and swam back to his group of friends. He probably did it on a dare, Fah thought. She hurried her paddle, not wanting to tow more children as if she were public transportation. Her stomach was empty and she did not want to waste the little energy she had left. She turned the boat down a familiar street and followed the aroma of turmeric and curry powder.

The market rose out of the destructive flood like a life-saving island. The shops, carrying goods from towns untouched by devastation, were raised high on platforms in makeshift grids. Rice in various states sat in large basins. Mounds of colorful fruits and vegetables, lower in quality and variety than pre-flood time, were appreciated and caressed like precious jewels. Fish, fresh from the river, wiggled in fishermen's boats, waiting to be sold.

The flood had not dampened the spirit of the market. There was a music to this place—twittering and chattering—a disorganized orchestra of sounds. The melodic singing of the sellers advertising their goods. The yelling of discourse. The sizzling of noodles in woks on small clay stoves. Laughter. Before the war and the flood, she would have reveled in the market like a bee collecting nectar. But as it was, with only half the money needed for the items on her mother's list, this place was now a battle ground.

Even though her father still had a job, money was tight because everything was expensive. Once, she overheard him telling her mom that the Thai Baht was losing its value after the government was pressured to reduce its price to trade with the Yen. Each time her mom pulled out the thinning coin purse she hid in her bosom, Fah could see the strain on her face.

Knowing she could not afford chicken meat, she bargained for bones. It would be the base for soup. At the vegetable stall, she whispered for the discarded, the peel. In her mother's hands they would be diced and stewed until one could no longer see their origin. The only thing she could not negotiate for was rice. Whatever the country was able to produce had to go to the Japanese troops first, leaving the people with what was left. So she bought the imperfects, the chipped and broken pieces abandoned on the ground after the milling process.

Despite telling herself to stay away, her boat made its way as if by its own will to her favorite section—the aisle of florists. An array of cheerful flowers overwhelmed both sides of what was once a pathway. Here, the air was sweeter. She breathed it in, filling her lungs with its optimism.

She stopped her boat in front of a stall. From its rafters and the edges of umbrellas, a thick curtain of jasmine garlands hung. On the platform, mini roses leaned on each other like exhausted dancers in water-filled jars. Lotus flowers, with stems cut off, floated in clay pots. Mounds of marigolds piled high like treasure inside a king's coffer.

No seller greeted her. The stall appeared unmanned. Fah noticed a lone jasmine garland sprawling at the edge of the platform, neglected like a baby bird fallen from its nest. It must have dropped from the rafter above. She picked it up and brought it to her nose. The sweet smell, once as familiar as her own, tugged at her heart. There was a jasmine shrub outside her window. The wind used to carry the scent into her bedroom each night, lulling her to sleep. It was drowned now, flowerless. Her nights had been restless without it. She wondered if anyone would notice the garland missing. It was so small and there were so many.

"That's pretty," a voice said from the platform.

Startled, Fah looked up. A woman emerged through the curtains of hanging flowers. She looked unusual. While her face was youthful, she had a head full of gray hair. Her scent was even stranger. Even amongst the flowers, the girl could smell the fragrance emanating from her. Minty. Sweet. Anise-like. Warm. Lemony. Woodsy. Pungent. Green. It was the oddest combination of scents she had ever encountered.

Fah placed the garland back on the platform.

"You don't want it?" the woman asked.

The girl smiled weakly. "I don't have any money. Sorry."

"Then just take it."

"What?"

The woman leaned down, picked up the garland and handed it to her. "Just don't tell the owner."

"You're not the owner?"

"She's sick. I'm only helping for the day. She won't mind. Just take it."

Fah wanted the garland, but she shook her head. She did not know why except she had a feeling that if she had accepted it, life would somehow turn out differently.

The woman looked at her with penetrating eyes. Finally, she said, "Could you consider it a deposit?"

"For what?"

"I need to hire a boat for tomorrow."

"Oh! But that's not what I do."

"I'll pay you the same amount I would a professional boatman."

"Really?" Fah blurted. "But I'm just a girl."

The woman's face puckered as if she had just eaten something sour. "Rubbish. That's no excuse."

Fah thought of her two little sisters. They were growing quickly, and often her mother had to forgo food so they could eat. She wished to lift her parents' burden, even if just a little.

"What do I need to do?" she asked.

"Take me from place to place. Nowhere far. Maybe help me carry some things. Nothing more than you can handle."

"How do I know you won't sell me to the Japanese?"

The woman laughed. The sound was hearty for her petite body, attracting the attention of those nearby.

"I like your spirit. What's your name?" she asked.

"Fah."

"Like the sky or the color?"

"Both, I suppose."

"Well, my name is Mali. I'm a healer from Kampong Java. Do you know where that is?"

Fah nodded. She knew the neighborhood. The people there were immigrants from the Dutch East Indies. It was not too far from her house.

The gray-haired woman continued, "Although I'm not one of them, everyone there knows me. I helped deliver most of the babies in that neighborhood in the last twenty years. And I'm no admirer of the Japanese."

Fah looked at the gray-haired woman. Her mother told her she could tell whether a person is trustworthy from their eyes. All she needed to do was look for kindness.

"So, should I pick you up here tomorrow?" Fah asked and took the garland.

"Come to my house. I live opposite the Muslim cemetery. There are several large mango trees in the front, you can't miss it. At about three in the afternoon."

Fah arrived at the old Thai house before her scheduled appointment. Made entirely of golden teak, it sat high on four stilts surrounded by the flood. The water covered its entire yard, drowning trees and gardens. The only way in or out of the house was by a set of tall stairs in the front that were half way under water. The rest of the building was untouched, as if up there the plight of the city was but an earthly trouble.

It was the prettiest house she had ever seen. Glazed clay tiles in a pattern of fish scales covered the high pitched roof. The paneled walls leaned out at a slight angle like a book being opened. Hanging along the eaves of the roof were orchid plants, stems laden with pink and orange blooms cascading down like a woman's earrings.

"Hello," she hollered.

A minute later, Mali came to the railing.

"You're early. I'm still getting ready. Why don't you come up?" she yelled and disappeared.

Fah tied her boat to the lowest stair rail and climbed the steep steps. The stairs led to an expansive porch, covered entirely by the roof. Many colorful futons peppered the floor next to a short-legged wood table. To the right and the back of the porch were what Fah assumed to be the kitchen and the bedrooms. The wood doors to each had carved images of women. Some were bare-chested like the female celestials on temple wall murals. In one corner, several bunches of bananas on a large stalk almost as tall as she leaned against a wall.

Fah liked it here. The warm honey-toned wood. The openness of the porch. The way every piece of furniture sat low on the ground as if prostrating to their god that was the house.

She could not see Mali anywhere and assumed she must be behind one of the doors. It appeared, from the silence of the house, the gray-haired woman lived alone. That was very unusual. Nobody else Fah knew lived that way.

On a spot on the floor, she noticed a small boat-shaped basket made of banana leaf and filled with various flowers. She walked to it and picked it up. The colors were beautiful—red, yellow, white, blue. They reminded her of the aisle of florists. The jasmine garland Mali had given her was now on her pillow and sweetened her sleep last night. Perhaps, she thought, these flowers were to help someone sleep. She placed it back where she found it.

Finally, a door at the far end of the house opened. Mali came out with a bamboo basket in her hand. She was wearing a long striped skirt that almost reached her ankles and a white blouse cinched at her waist. Her gray hair was gathered at the nape of her neck in a neat bun. She looked regal, like an aristocratic woman. Fah felt herself staring too long and shifted her eyes instead to the bunches of bananas in the corner.

"They're magic bananas," the woman said.

"Sorry?"

"For stomachaches and female ailments. Very potent. Grab some for me, will you?"

The bananas looked like any Fah could find at the market. Nothing about them, at least from what she could see, looked magical.

"The ripest ones, please," Mali said. "People don't like the bitter taste of the unripe ones."

"How many?"

"Six will do."

The girl picked the yellowest, softest bananas, and handed them to Mali who put them in the bamboo basket. Fah caught a glimpse of pouches in various colors and odd accoutrements inside.

"Where would you like me to take you today?" Fah asked.

"I have to make a couple of house visits to my patients."

"You said you're a healer. Is that like being a doctor?"

"Not exactly. But I help them, those within my power, just the same."

The first house was on Sathon Road, a main throughway in their district. It was two-story, like Fah's, but that was where the similarities ended. Painted the color of preserved lemons with overhanging red tiled roofs and an abundance of glass windows, the stately home sat on a knoll on a large estate. Looking up at the mansion, she felt small and under-dressed.

There was a man wearing a sarong waiting at the bottom of the knoll when they arrived. He pulled the boat in by its bow and tied it to a wood pole fixed deep in the ground.

"Hello, Abdul," Mali said and turned to Fah. "He's the groundskeeper here."

"Hello," the girl said.

"How's your wife and the new baby?" the healer asked.

"Mariam is recovering quickly," he said. "And the baby is keeping her busy. Whenever she cries, everyone in the kampong can hear."

"That means she'll be strong."

The man laughed. "Mariam made some vegetable curry this morning. I'll bring it by for dinner."

"I'd love that."

"The lady is waiting for you in the sitting room."

"Thank you."

Fah followed Mali on the makeshift wood plank walkway that led to the house.

A young girl, not much older than Fah, greeted them at the front door and showed them to the light-filled room in one corner of the house. In the middle of the room sat a woman on a chaise lounge. She was beautiful, with shiny black hair and pale yellow skin. She stretched out a hand toward Mali.

"Thanks for coming on short notice, doctor," she said, her voice barely above a whisper.

Her delicate features were contorted with pain. Mali introduced her as Khun Sai.

"My headache won't go away," Khun Sai said, her eyes watering.

Fah lowered herself onto the floor until Mali gestured her to sit on one of the chairs next to a shiny wood table. She watched as Mali examined the woman, touching her forehead and wrists.

The same girl who showed them in brought a tray of tea and sweets and placed them on the shiny table. Fah stared at the food with wide eyes. Each was presented on a small plate with tiny pink roses painted as if by mice. On one were *luk chup*, a colorful mung bean-filled dessert shaped into mini fruits and vegetables. On another were *tako*, layered coconut pudding in cups made of banana leaf. The last plate had her favorite—*tong yod*, sweet egg yolk drops cooked in syrup. Sugar was a rarity since the war had started and she could not remember the last time she had seen dessert.

After Mali had nodded her approval, Fah chose a piece of golden *tong yod*. It broke into jasmine-scented stars in her mouth and her face broke into a smile.

"The last time I prescribed you crushed ginger root boiled with warm water. Is that right?" Mali asked.

Khun Sai nodded.

"Did it help?"

"Yes, but it keeps coming back. I haven't been able to sleep."

"Did you just have your period?"

"Yes. How did you know?"

Mali smiled. "You need your aura cleansed. I'm going to need a cup of hot water."

The maid, who had been waiting in a corner, walked with quiet feet to the kitchen. When she returned, she brought with her a cup with steam rising off it. Mali took it and dropped a pinch of dried flowers in. They bloomed as they touched the bottom. She handed the cup to her patient and lit the end of a dry herb bundle until white smoke emanated from it.

"Please drink," she said and got up from her seat.

Khun Sai sipped from the cup while Mali waved the burning herbs around her body. She mumbled words the girl could not comprehend.

Soon, the patient's face relaxed. "Oh doctor, you're a miracle worker!"

Mali poured the same dried flowers onto a measuring apparatus. When satisfied with the amount, she placed them in a pouch and handed it to Khun Sai.

"Take this," Mali said. "For a week before your next menstrual cycle, put a little bit in hot water to make tea. Come to my house when you run out. Or you can send Abdul."

"Thank you!" Khun Sai squeezed Mali's hand. No longer in pain, she turned her attention to Fah. "Is this your new helper, doctor?"

Mali smiled. "This is Fah. Like the sky and the color."

"What grade are you in?" asked Khun Sai.

Fah swallowed. "Oh, I'm not in school. But before it closed down I was in tenth grade."

"That's right…the war is not kind to anyone, is it?" she said. Her eyes turned sad. "You're a beautiful girl. My daughter would have been your age, had she…"

Mali reached over and squeezed her hand.

Khun Sai wiped her eye and said, "Oh, please have some more, Fah. I love making desserts but my husband doesn't care for them. He thinks they're wasteful. But I find them cheery. And we all need a little bit of that in this time, don't you think?"

"How's the minister?" the healer asked.

"He's been busy with work lately preparing official visits with the Japanese officers, arranging speeches and the like. We haven't had dinner together since before the flood."

After Fah ate her fill and the adults conversed on current events, Khun Sai handed Mali an envelope and saw them to the front door.

"Thank you, truly, doctor. My husband will be happy to see I'm no longer a grouch."

"Please send my regards to the minister."

"Of course."

At the make-shift dock, Abdul untied Fah's boat and helped them in.

"Please remind Mariam to drink the herbal tea I gave her," said Mali, "It'll help with the milk."

"Yes, doctor."

In the boat, while Mali fiddled with the contents inside her basket, Fah stole a moment to adjust her skirt. Her stomach was not used to so much food in one sitting.

"How did you fix Khun Sai with just flowers and herbs?" Fah asked. "Was that—witchcraft?"

Mali laughed. "Avicenna, a Persian scholar from the eleventh century defined medicine as the science by which we learn the various states of the human body in health and when not in health, and the means by which health is likely to be lost, and when lost, is likely to be restored. I just learned over the years the keys to maintaining health. It's true that sometimes I consult the magical realm, but only sparingly. One should always approach that world with caution. Most people can be cured simply with things of this world. And sometimes by the power of their own mind. In Khun Sai's case, she didn't need much more than a clean aura and medicinal plants."

"You studied medicine?"

"I wanted to be a doctor when I was younger. But the medical school only accepted women into the nursing program. And so I learned to be a nurse. I practiced for a bit. But I found it to be…restrictive. Not every ailment can be fixed with western medicine. Some need a combination of both eastern and western treatments. Others require something more—supernatural. With this job, I can do as I see fit with my patients. Even if I'm not a doctor, I get to help people."

"Khun Sai called you a doctor."

"It makes them feel better—the patients—calling me a doctor gives what I do credibility. It lets them believe I can help them just as well as the real doctor they can't afford."

"But you did help Khun Sai."

"While some, like her, still believe in the magical realm, more people are beginning to disregard it. So even if they can see proof, they will find other reasons to explain it. I'm a healer first. At least that's what I try to be. It matters less to me how I do it, or by which title."

The boat glided past an old Buddhist temple dating back to the Ayutthaya period. The *wat* had a Chinese junk-shaped *chedi* built by King Rama III, which Fah found to be oddly appropriate considering the flood. In the same moment, as if planned, she and Mali pressed their palms together, prayer-like, and bowed toward the temple and the Buddha statue residing within its walls.

They arrived at the house that belonged to Lung Tee, a butcher Fah knew from the market she frequented. Inside, the entire floor was raised above the water, cutting the height of the room in half. In it, Fah felt as though she was a giant.

The butcher was lying on a bed on a platform. He was shirtless, his skin red from fever. He reminded Fah of the beef he sold at his stall. His wife and two sons kneeled on either side of him, their faces leaden with concern.

"It's my stomach. It hurts. The pain won't go away," Lung Tee said, his hands clutching at his middle as if to prevent his insides from spilling out.

Mali pressed her palms on his torso. He winced as if she was prodding him with a hot iron. It did not matter how gently she pressed or where, he was in agony. Her face turned paler the longer she examined him.

"How long has it been like this?" Mali asked.

"The pain started a few months back, but it only got really bad these last few weeks," Lung Tee said, his voice strained as if all the energy had left him.

"Can you help him?" his wife asked.

Mali did not answer. Instead, she pulled out a small glass bottle of clear liquid and unscrewed the cap. She inserted a dropper into it and extracted the liquid.

"Open your mouth, please," she said and squeezed the clear elixir onto Lung Tee's tongue.

The butcher's face unwound. He closed his eyes. Soon after, his jagged breathing became slow and steady.

Mali handed the entire bottle to his wife. "Use this tincture. One milliliter every four hours for the pain. No more—that's very important. There's enough here for seven days. Send your son to my house next week if your husband still has the need for more."

"Thank you, doctor."

One of the sons handed a wrapped package to Mali. The paper wrapping had red splotches in places. *Blood.*

"Please accept this as payment," the wife said.

"It's okay," Mali answered. "Keep it."

The butcher's wife placed her hand on Mali's. "Please."

Mali nodded and handed the package to Fah, who realized it was a piece of beef.

Back in the boat, Mali emptied her sigh as if it were a heavy cargo she had been carrying. A cloud of melancholy spread out like a funeral shawl, weighing down the vessel. Fah watched as the healer dipped her hand into the river, parting it, leaving a wake behind her. A raft of purple-flowered hyacinths floated past them. A white crane stood on the raft like a soldier at attention. His eyes, like Mali's, were on the river.

"You should take the beef home," the healer said, breaking the silence.

"You don't want it?"

"I don't have a need for it. People in Kampong Java bring me food on a daily basis. So I never have to cook. I think they take pity on me for being a single woman."

"You don't have any family?"

"My parents passed at about the same time I graduated from nursing school. As for my sister, well, she too is gone. And I'm afraid this life is not suitable for marriage."

"Why not?"

"Oh, so many reasons. None of which you'd understand."

"I'm fifteen. I'm old enough to understand many things."

"Age has nothing to do with it. Only someone like me who deals with the magical realm would know. And there aren't many of us. At least no one nearby."

"How did you learn about that world?"

"I was born into it. My mother, my sister, me—we all have it in our blood."

"Your mother taught you?"

Mali nodded.

"So do you know what's wrong with Lung Tee?" Fah asked.

"He has a growth inside his body. Large enough to feel with my hands," she said.

"A growth? Of what?"

"Sometimes a body produces a mass inside. Sometimes that mass poisons the body, cannibalizing the good part and turning it bad."

"How did he get it?"

Mali shook her head. "I don't know."

"Will he survive?"

"There isn't much I can do for him. The masses are in his vital organs. Maybe if he had come to me earlier…it's hard to tell. Right now, all I can do is help ease his pain. The medicine I gave was a strong pain killer."

"You can't use magic?"

She shook her head. "Not for this."

"Why didn't you tell him?"

"I wanted him to spend the last month of his life not worrying about death. The medication should ease his pain enough to make him feel almost normal. He'll have a comfortable death at least. Many people can't even count on that. Living next to a cemetery and doing what I do, you come to an understanding very quickly that nothing can stop death."

Fah realized then that the healer had probably witnessed more deaths than most had in one lifetime. Each person Mali had tried to save and lost were like a battle scar on her soul. She wondered if, to the healer, the war was just another way to lose them. Another way to feel helpless.

A cool wind swept through, drying the sweat on Fah's forehead. From her perspective, the world appeared to be covered entirely by water—an eye filled with tears.

People are adaptable beings. After the second month of living with the flood, the inhabitants of Bangkok had learned to not only cope but thrive. They grew vegetables in pots hanging from rafters. They made a diet out of fish and shrimp from the river. Some even started businesses around the flood.

Mali became Fah's regular customer—her only customer. People continued to get sick, die, give birth, and so the healer had someone to visit every day. In a month, Fah had seen a total of five births, one death, ten skin rashes, three dysentery cases, and a myriad of other ailments. She had become quite attached to the healer, seeing how she cared for her patients, sometimes not taking anything more than a bowl of jasmine water to quench her thirst. The way Mali healed, Fah could not tell which part was medicine and which part was magic. She came to view them as one.

"Can you teach me? To do what you do?" Fah asked the healer while she was home bundling herbs. It took her a week to gather enough courage to ask the question.

"No."

Fah felt blood leaving her face.

"Let me explain," said Mali. "What I do, the way I do it, requires more than just medical knowledge. That, you can learn at nursing school. The other part needs something more innate. And I'm afraid I don't see it in you. And even if you had it, this is not the life you want."

"Why not? You do it."

"I don't see you here, Fah. You belong somewhere else, with someone else. In a different life. In that place you'll find your happiness."

"But you're happy. In your own way. I want that."

"You only see what I allow you to see, my dear girl. There's a dangerous side to this life."

"Whatever it is, it can't be that bad."

Mali shook her head. "You're a stubborn girl, aren't you?"

"That's what my mom tells me."

Fah could feel the healer's intense eyes on her. She seemed to be turning a thought over in her head, trying to arrive at a conclusion. The girl stared back just as intensely. She wanted Mali to know she was serious. There were not many options for a girl like her with a limited education and no means to get more. After the flood, there would still be the war. What if school was no longer in her future? A healer's life, like Mali's, was the best she could hope for.

"Perhaps you need to see it. The darker side of what I do," Mali said, finally.

"I can handle it."

"Then come with me to the Chinese neighborhood near the river."

"What's there?"

"Something very important."

Fah had never paddled that far before. And there had been rumors coming out of that place—stories of disappearances. Of men who had disagreed a little too loudly with the war. Of pretty women who walked home too late. The Chinese were the subject of the worst treatment by the Japanese soldiers. But she could not pass up the chance to prove to Mali that she could deal with every aspect of this life.

"Alright. When?"

"Before tomorrow's dawn. Three in the morning."

The girl swallowed. "Does it have to be in the dark?"

Mali scoffed. "Already, you're afraid."

Fah felt blood rushing to her face. "Only of my parents finding out."

"We can remedy that," the healer said and walked into the kitchen. A moment later she came out with a pouch and handed it to Fah.

"What is it?" the girl asked.

"Place it under your pillow when you leave. They won't know you're gone."

Fah clutched at the pouch, wondering what kind of magic was coiling within.

Under the cloak of darkness, everything looked sinister. As she paddled past a Thai Buddhist temple, the hair on her neck stood up. This happened every time. It was the tree—a great and ancient Bodhi tree with dense leaves that spanned the length of a field near the entrance of the temple. Its bark was covered with several squares of thin gold leaf. Around its immense trunk were wrapped fabrics in many colors, it looked like the end of a rainbow. But instead of evoking happiness, it stirred a sense of foreboding. It was the smell. There was a perpetual scent of burning incense surrounding it, as if leaking from its pores.

People believed spirits lived in the tree. The gold leaf and the colorful cloths were their offerings. Fah willed herself not to look at the ominous tree. Instead, she focused her eyes on the bow of her boat and the rhythm of her paddling.

The moon was a round white ball above, bathing her skin silver. She imagined herself spinning a cocoon with its light, pulling it around her like a blanket. Soon, she arrived at the healer's house. Mali was standing at the bottom of the stairs with her bamboo basket. There was another boat tied to the handrail.

"Whose is that?" Fah asked as soon as she was close enough to be heard.

"A back-up. I wasn't certain if you'd come. Timing is of the essence."

Fah wanted to be angry at the healer, but she was not even sure if she would come until she did. She had talked herself in and out of it a hundred times that night. Her hands were shaky when she put the pouch under her pillow, and only then did she feel brave enough to leave.

She grabbed the bamboo basket from Mali's hand. It was lighter than usual. The doctor did not have her contraptions and pouches in it.

"This is not a medical visit, is it?" Fah asked.

Mali did not answer.

"You not trusting me is beginning to really bother me," Fah said.

"In time, you'll learn that while some things are better left unsaid, other things can never be said at all," the healer said as she stepped into the boat.

Fah paddled the boat toward the Chao Phraya. Even in this witching hour, there were vessels out on the river. Fishermen's boats were returning from the night's work at sea. Others, just beginning their work day, were casting nets into the water. The houseboats of the river gypsies bobbled up and down with the waves. The gypsies, accustomed to life on the water, were probably the only ones whose lives were not seriously affected by the flood. A cool wind rushed through from the direction of the Gulf and Fah wished for something warm.

"Turn here," Mali said, breaking the silence they had inhabited since they left her house.

Fah turned down a creek and it led them to a neighborhood of three-story concrete buildings. She had been here before the war and almost did not recognize it. The streets that were once bustling with stores on the first floor, selling toys, old books, clothing, food, and gold, appeared deserted, and not just from slumber.

"Right here," said Mali, her voice lowered to a whisper. "Then left over there."

They turned up one small alley after another until Fah could not tell which way was north. Around them, the eerie quietude mocked, reminding her something was amiss.

"Stop at that store ahead. The one with the gold sign," Mali said. The writing was in Chinese, a language Fah could not understand even though she was half Chinese by blood.

The girl guided the boat in the direction the healer pointed. She stopped next to the steps and tied her boat to a wooden post. Luckily, the building was high enough above the street that no water entered the main floor. The front door, made of wood panels folded like an accordion, was partially open.

"You need to come inside with me. It's not safe out here. Even with the flood, the Japanese still patrol this area," said Mali.

Fah shivered at the thought of being caught at night by a soldier. She had heard horrible stories and did not wish to be one of them. She followed Mali into the building.

Inside, the entire place smelled like rotted trees—musty and pungent. There was only one light source, a single hurricane lantern. Fah almost screamed when she noticed a person, an old man, sitting next to it. Toothless, his wrinkly face looked as if it had collapsed in on itself. But it was not the most terrible thing about it. His eye sockets were empty.

"He's blind and doesn't speak," Mali whispered. "But he knows every herb by scent."

The old man got up and shuffled to them. Without words, he handed Mali the lantern. Fah could now see the mountains of herbs around her. Some were in baskets and some were in glass cases. Roots that looked like human bodies, dried flowers and leaves, powders in shades of brown and yellow. In one corner was a red shrine with burning incense.

The deeper they went into the innards of the house, the quieter it became. It was the first time Fah had ever been inside a concrete home. Concrete on the outside, concrete on the inside, concrete in between. There were no other doors or windows except the one she went through. It was cool, cave-like, with moisture beading on the walls.

"What are we doing here?" the girl whispered.

No answer came from Mali.

They walked until they reached the back of the building. There, a

45

set of stairs climbed into a tunnel of black.

"You can wait down here or go up with me. It's your choice," Mali said.

Neither option sounded good to Fah, but she did not want to be without the lantern nor the healer. Following behind, she glided her hands along the wall like eyes reading a map. Their footsteps echoed against the hard concrete. When they reached the second story, she heard sounds. It was the whispering of many voices. They grew louder the further they went, and Fah had the impression of walking toward a bee hive. Suddenly, they stopped.

They arrived in front of a doorway with curtains made of thick fabric the color of dried blood. The warmth of light was behind it. Fah could feel a manic energy in the air. It bounced off the walls—little bubbles filled with anxiety and anticipation—threatening to pop.

"Wait here," Mali said and handed her the lantern. "Whatever you hear, whatever happens inside or outside this room, do not come in."

She grabbed the basket from Fah's hand and walked through the curtains. Before they closed, Fah caught a glimpse inside. People were sitting huddled together on the floor. Many people. Their faces were in shadows. She wondered who they were and why Mali had come here.

In the dark corridor where she waited, the air was still and thick with humidity. The only light source came from the hurricane lantern, which seemed to be dimming and retreating as if chased by shadows. There was no sound except for her breathing and the dripping of the concrete walls. But there was a smell of something burning. Something organic, like a mixture of dry leaves and hair. It grew until it became overwhelming, making her head swim. Her legs and arms felt heavy, as were her eyelids. She slid onto the floor and leaned against the wall. There was a shifting—of the air around her, within her—and she lurched forward.

Colors danced in her vision. White, red, yellow, blue. Her palms tingled. Heat rose off of them as if they were the horizon from which the sun was rising. She lifted her hands to her face and saw the skin melting off of them like candle wax. The hair on her head was twirling and pirouetting like windblown branches on a tree. But she was not afraid. What she felt wasn't fear, but giddiness—a sense of hope.

A ruckus from below startled her. She heard them—dozens of feet against the concrete floor, marching to a steady rhythm. Japanese soldiers! She realized then that they were here for the people. Hope was quickly replaced by fear. She had an urgent desire to go through the curtains to the safety of the healer, but she remembered the warning.

The steps were coming closer. She pushed herself off of the floor and stumbled down the corridor, away from the direction of the stairs. In the dark, the long passage appeared endless. It was lined on both sides with doorways covered by curtains the color of night. By instinct, she knew she could not go through any of them. The footsteps kept coming closer. She wanted to scream but she knew she could not. Her voice would give them away. And so she kept silent as she traveled down the unending hallway.

A hand grabbed her shoulder. She whipped back and saw Mali. The healer touched her forehead and a cool, calmness radiated through her veins. The fog inside her head cleared.

"You can come back now," Mali said.

Fah blinked. "What's going on? Where are the soldiers?"

"There are no soldiers. At least not here in this moment."

"But I heard them. They were coming up to take away the people."

"They won't. You didn't let them. And they can't now."

"What happened?"

"I'm sorry, but I had to see whether it was really there."

"What?"

"Magic."

"I don't understand."

"I had my suspicions. But I couldn't risk unlocking it until you were ready. There's magic inside you, dear girl."

Fah felt as if she was still asleep, or whatever state she was in a moment earlier. She could not believe her ears. The healer said there was magic inside her.

"Let's leave," Mali said.

Fah noticed the healer looked drained and pale as if she had been suffering through many sleepless nights. As she normally did, the girl grabbed the bamboo basket from her hand. Its weight almost tipped her over. She opened the basket and saw it filled to the brim with stones nestled together, one on top of another.

The healer offered no explanation, but this time Fah knew the answer. Mali was right. While some things were better left unsaid, some could never be said at all.

They climbed down the dark stairs. At the front of the building, the blind man was waiting for them. In his opened palm was a bracelet. Gold.

Without words, he thrust it in front of Mali's face.

"I'm not doing this for money," said the healer.

The man would not move.

"Alright. I'll give it to her then," Mali said. She picked up the bracelet and put it around Fah's wrist before she could protest. "It will remind you of this day."

Fah placed the bamboo basket into the boat before climbing in. With the stones, the boat felt heavier. Yet, Fah did not mind. She knew the cargo was precious.

Her arms, stronger than she had remembered, pulled the paddle through the water, propelling them forward faster than ever before. Buildings and trees whizzed past. Her heart was as light as the wings of butterflies.

At the bottom step of the old Thai house on stilts, Mali and Fah looked at each other as if they were seeing the other clearly for the first time. The girl handed the healer the bamboo basket and Mali accepted it with both hands. The healer turned to climb up the stairs, then paused.

"I'll teach you what I know," Mali said.

"Really? You will?"

"But as I said before, this life is not for you. You belong somewhere else. But I'll share what I have and you can do with it as you wish," she said. Then she walked up the stairs, leaving Fah to ponder her words.

Above, the sky was changing as the night prepared its retreat. It seemed the water, too, was beginning to ebb. Soon, Fah knew, it would return to the Chao Phraya and the war would resume. But she was not afraid.

# Call me Blue

California Desert, U.S.A., 1994

My grandmother used to say the only thing standing in the way of a stranger becoming a friend is an introduction. You can call me Blue. I don't usually hitch a ride like this but I don't really have a choice. As you may have already noticed, having just stopped to eat here, this place is pretty much nowhere. So you're the best chance I have of getting out.

This is an odd little town. I know. It was founded by a romantic man who ran out of gas. He was a rich man from the east coast who drove across the country for a dream. He had planned to go down the coast to San Diego, but he stopped for a refill in our town, just a passthrough road then, and never left. If you've seen both San Diego and our neck of the woods, you'd know that they are nothing alike. You could say that the east coast man had settled in every sense of the word. I suppose if you had been traveling on a dusty washboard road for weeks, the middle of nowhere was good enough.

My grandmother doesn't believe it was coincidence that led the east coast man to this town. She said he was meant to be here, just as she was. While it's difficult for me to imagine how this place would have looked through the eyes of someone who had never seen it before, I suppose its impossibly blue sky and raw honey-colored mountain range could be considered beautiful—in that bare, hollow way—a place one could fill with possibilities.

50

Even though no one quite knew what the east coast man's dream was, the entire town honored him by putting his name on every-thing—schools, a library, a baseball field, a hybrid snake designed by the local snake breeder. My school even has a picture of him in a glass cabinet. In it, he's standing next to a Model T, wearing a three-piece suit, and surrounded by an orange grove. The trees were deceptive, really. Aside from them, the town is a desert—as brown and desolate as any drought-ridden landscape in Southern California.

Sometimes I wonder if he had never founded the town, whether it would have been founded at all. It sits inside a valley dimpled by a bone-dry lake bed and surrounded by rocky mountains that my father calls the Devil's Bowl. The real name of the town, Lake Beryl, is a lot less ominous—unless you think irony threatening. Which apparently many people did. It has been tracking negative on population since the seventies. I suspect the people who left all drove south to San Diego.

My family owns that restaurant you just ate at. It's been serving fusion food since before it became a trend. The menu includes Mexican, Thai, Chinese, and American. The real reason for our schizophrenic repertoire has less to do with trends than survival and indecision. My grandmother is Thai-Chinese and my grandfather was Mexican-American. Each is as proud as the other of their heritage.

They met, like many mixed-race couples of their time, in an ESL class. My grandfather was teaching it. Grandma, *Yah,* as I call her, likes telling me stories about how my grandfather would give her terrible grades just so he could tutor her after school. I told her that would have gotten him fired nowadays, but she just laughed.

Somehow, along the way they decided having a restaurant was the best thing for their family. They were right of course. In a town where the unemployment rate hovered between abysmal and laughable, my dad, his two brothers, and all their wives always had a job and we kids never went hungry a day in our lives.

For a restaurant in the middle of nowhere, we've always had steady customers. We're far enough from everywhere else that people stop here for the same reason the east coast man did—to fill up their gas tanks and stomachs. Because our parents are always working, I spent a lot of time at the restaurant with my four cousins: Leila, Gabriella, Anika, and Maria. We made up a lot of games to kill boredom. In one game, we guessed the food the out-of-towners would order. I usually won.

My method is this:

1) San Diegans usually order Mexican food (particularly *carne asada*), then they complain about how theirs is better.

2) College students like to order a pancake breakfast with extra bacon in the afternoon.

3) White retirees tend to order Chinese and ask for extra crispy noodles in their egg drop soup.

4) Women with expensive purses like to order Thai food, hold the onions.

I can't tell you the reasons to my method, only that they worked. I won so many times my cousins accused me of cheating. How they thought I could cheat at a guessing game, I don't know. Although despite their accusations, they still played the game with me. And before you ask, yes, I guessed what you would order—and I was right.

Leila and Gabriella are sisters and so are Anika and Maria. I'm an only child. My parents divorced when I was six and Dad never remarried or had any more children. I'm glad he didn't. He has a horrible track record when it comes to naming babies.

The name on my birth certificate reads Fah-ying. I hate it. I've since forgiven him because his reason was honorable. It's Yah's name. Its meaning in Thai, "celestial princess," is nice. Although the name suites my free-spirited grandma, I've never seen myself as such. Luckily some Thai words can be translated to more than one thing. So, its literal meaning, *fah* for 'blue', and *ying* for 'woman,' was more to my liking. The Blue Woman of Lake Beryl—like a classic horror movie.

But this being America, the name when written phonetically needs a hyphen. Any future parents should take note that giving their kids a hyphenated name is cruel. Nobody, and I mean no one ever born in the history of our town, has had a hyphenated name (my grandmother came from Thailand, so she doesn't count). I don't appreciate being the first and last of the hyphenated, so I tell everyone to call me Blue.

Luckily, no one seemed to mind except for Grandpa. He loved his wife so much that he thought my disliking her name was an insult to her. But he's dead now so it doesn't matter anymore. Plus, Yah doesn't mind. She calls me Fah, like her nickname, so we're both happy with the arrangement.

There's not much I could do to anger her. I'm her favorite of all the granddaughters. She may even like me more than her own kids. At first, I thought it was because I look like a *hapa* version of her with lighter hair and eyes. Or maybe it's because we share a name. I didn't find out the real reason until much later, when it was almost too late.

When I said it didn't matter to me that Grandpa didn't like that I changed my name, I didn't mean it disrespectfully. My family is big on respect. My dad and uncles will kill a person for disrespecting them. At least that's what they say. I can't confirm whether it's true, but I doubt anyone ever crossed them. Each one is at least six-foot-three and as wide as a Samoan linebacker. While my grandmother was proud of her giant breed of boys, she used to lament that no one would dare marry her granddaughters for fear of their fathers. My dad and uncles all find this amusing.

The kids at my high school think we're rich. The only reason for that is our house. We live in a large compound on top of a hill with its own road. My grandfather's father built it with his own hands when the land was nothing more than dry scrub and boulders. Most of it is a citrus grove now, all started from a graft of a tree my grandmother smuggled in from Thailand. Over the years, the main house was expanded, and more buildings were added to fit the growing family. My dad and I live in one of the small cottages on the grounds converted from a horse stable, while my uncles and their families are in the main house.

After my grandfather passed away, Yah moved out of the main house and into the other small cottage with its own kitchen and bathroom. She was weird about her privacy (for reasons I would later find out), but she enjoyed getting visits from me and my cousins. We took turns going there regularly at night before bed—at first because our fathers ordered us to, but later because we really liked spending time with her. Sometimes we would bring our blankets and pillows over to her cottage and sleep on the floor to hear stories about her life as a girl in Thailand.

Whenever Yah told us about her childhood, her sweet eyes looked as if they were seeing into another realm. In those moments, she was most beautiful. My grandmother is a beautiful woman regardless of whether she is reminiscing, even after the suppleness of her skin and the shininess of her hair were stolen by age. She has high cheekbones, skin the color of antique ivory, and the gait of a dancer. Yet, she said she had no lover until she met my grandfather. I asked if her father was as big as mine, and she laughed.

Yah laughs a lot. It's my favorite thing about her. That, and her hair. She has the longest hair of any woman I know. During the day, she keeps her silky locks coiled on top of her head like a turban. Over the years, while the women her age droop over like dying flowers, she stands at the same height because whatever she lost in bones, she gained in hair. At night, she would let it down and spread it over her like a blanket, as white as goose down. She would then spend an hour brushing it. She never let me touch her hair though. Thais do not like anyone touching their heads. For the most part they are a superstitious group of people, Yah said.

Her childhood was a thousand times more interesting than mine. She grew up in Bangkok during the second world war, under Japanese occupation (the Thai government told its people to call the occupiers friends, but that's another story). Before you start feeling bad for her, she recalls her childhood with fondness. The war, for me, is a series of black and white images of flying bombers, dead bodies, and mushroom clouds. But if you had asked her, she would tell you she had a blast.

During the bombings by the Allies, her father would lower her and her siblings into a dry concrete culvert. As they waited for the attack to subside, he would feed them ghost stories while spooning dinner into their mouths. *Idyllic.*

My grandmother's path from that moment in the concrete culvert to the Devil's Bowl was indirect and, as she said, serendipitous. It was very much a 'being in the right place at the right time' situation. She knew someone, who knew someone, who knew something that was just the right thing to know. The someone she knew was a witch doctor, who knew a client who was married to the Minister of Education. After the war, he wanted to develop a strong partnership with America by sending many of the young people in his country to study abroad. Life took her by surprise, to say the least.

As surprising as Yah found her life to be, she is also full of surprises. I came upon one of them quite by accident. As far as I know, I am the only one in the family who has knowledge of it. An insomniac by blood (my dad told me my mom was too, but then he also called her by many names, some I cannot repeat here), I would walk the grounds of our compound whenever I couldn't sleep. My favorite place to go was the citrus grove, especially when the orange blossoms were blooming. One night, Yah was there.

At first, I thought she was a ghost. Naturally, I went closer for a look. I have never been afraid of ghosts. To me, they're more of a curiosity than something to be feared. They seem just like any human, but a lot less solid and a lot more shy. When I saw her, Yah was as radiant as the full moon above and as naked as the day she was born. Her hair, the only thing to shield her from the chilly air. She was, as best I can describe, drinking the moonlight. When she noticed I was there, she beckoned me over and told me her secret.

My grandmother learned magic from that same witch doctor she knew. Well, 'learned' is not quite the right word because you need to have the magic inside you. A better word would be 'unlocked'. Being a witch is about tapping into the sources of nature that allow you access into multiple realities. And in between those realities lives unimaginable power.

The multiple realities sit on top of each other like layers of a cake. Each layer is composed of a past, a present, and a future—with the past being the sponge base that holds up the flavorful present, while the future is unfixed and changeable like whipped topping. Between each of the layers of reality, however, is where supernatural things like spirits and monsters reside. Whenever Yah accesses this in-between place, she is magic.

For a long time, Yah would use magic for little things like healing her family members of cold viruses. Whenever someone was sick, she would use the herbs she grew in her garden to make medicine. But they were just delivery packages to hold her magic for consumption. It's a handy skill to have because everyone in my family hates going to the doctor. She also used it to make the 'secret ingredient' Dad thinks is MSG, which explains how our little place in the middle of nowhere gets repeat customers.

I asked her why she never told anyone else about her secret and she said it was for my grandfather. He was not a supporter of it, being Catholic and all. Since the witch doctor whom she apprenticed under was never married and told her being a witch was not a career suitable for a married woman, Yah made a promise on her wedding day to go on a hiatus. The things you do for love.

After her husband died, she figured he would not mind that she unchained her magic (death usually makes people more mellow). I could tell from the way she reveled in the moonlight that she missed being a witch, so I agreed to never tell anyone in my family about it. She never said anything about strangers, so as long as you promise not to tell my family, we should be good.

What Yah didn't know then was that when she decided to crank up her magic, mine would unlock. In full disclosure, she was aware there was some of her magic inside me. That was why she preferred my company. There's an affinity witches have toward one another, as if there's an invisible thread connecting them. What she did not know was how much magic I would have, or whether it would be anything worth telling me about.

There are people in the world on the cusp of magic who never went over to the other side. They appear as though they are exceptional at making guesses or having good instincts. They're like normal people but a touch luckier. For a long time, I fit the description of these 'cuspies' so Yah did not want to alarm me unnecessarily. She views magic a bit like a terminal disease.

So needless to say, on the day my magic unlocked, I was utterly unprepared. That morning, in first period Pre-Calculus, I remember getting this odd tingling feeling in my fingertips. By lunch it grew until my entire palms radiated with the heat. Panic stricken, I hid in the bathroom, washing and rewashing my hands with cold water until they turned to prunes. I wanted to leave, but I had an important test to take that day. Plus, the school was miles away from home and I didn't have a car. Walking the Devil's Bowl in a-hundred-degree heat was murderous, so I decided to take my chance with the burning palms.

I wish I had left. An 'F' and a third degree sunburn would have been better than what happened. I was sitting next to Warren Cooper, a big cheat. Usually I would situate myself a certain way so he could not see my answers. But being distracted, I had forgotten. So he cheated off my test. I got angry, naturally.

I don't remember all the details but the next thing I knew, Warren began to shriek at the top of his lungs while clutching at his eyes. The teacher thought it was a severe panic attack and sent him to the nurse's office. I had no idea what I did. I only knew I had something to do with it when he screamed bloody murder and ran away at the sight of me. He still will not look me in the eyes to this day. I would apologize, but I don't know what I did. Besides, I have a feeling he would rather pretend to forget about it. People are fragile in that way. I know what you're wondering. I'm not feeling any tingling on my fingertips at the moment, so please do not worry. Unless you plan to cheat off my test.

After that first incident, I felt ragged and drained for the rest of the day. When I got home, Yah saw me and I swear she looked as if she had seen the ghost of Grandpa. She dropped whatever it was she was holding. I remember the sound of it breaking, startling me out of my skin.

She said it was my aura. What was once a beautiful blue turned deep purple, like the color of a brewing thunderstorm. She sat me down and gave me the bad news. I think there was a shot glass of Tequila involved.

Since that day she devoted herself to educating me about witchcraft. How to open up my chakras to the energy flowing all around me; how to access it, pulling it in and throwing it out like a lasso; how to know the differences between when I am controlling it and when it is controlling me. The thing with magic is that it is powerful, volatile, and attractive. Very, very attractive. And not just to the person accessing it. Ghosts and spirits are also drawn to the energy since it is of their realm. So, I needed to learn to navigate it and protect myself, pronto!

First, there are so many misconceptions about witches. Yah said it's best to think of them as portals between one realm and another—deliverers of information that is sometimes useful. There are, of course, bad witches who use magic for evil means. While rare, they are narcissistic and like to make a big impression. They ruin it for everyone else. The way to try to understand this dichotomy, Yah said, was to look at it like a religion. Same source, different usages, and vary greatly depending on the person wielding the tool.

Second, regarding ghosts, there are too many around to ignore so you might as well learn to talk to them. It's very much like talking to a person, with a few exceptions. Some are friendlier than others. Some are nice. Some are a-holes. You just have to get over the fact that they are quite flighty and can disappear without warning. It can make conversations with them frustrating. But they are a well of knowledge. That is if you can get them to pause long enough to consider a conversation with you. I know what you're wondering.

Yes. But don't worry, most of them don't care about the living unless they're extremely angry or bored. Bored ghosts can be as damaging as the angry ones, and cause havoc just the same.

Third, while it may seem fun to be able to control a life's force—making leaves shrivel and dry, then turning them green, and back again—it can take a lot out of you. The first week I learned this skill, I noticed my first gray hair. Every time I use magic, I am trading something of myself away, a sacrifice to the in-between world. It's a way for nature to control us, I suppose. A check and balance, like the government.

Fourth, while the ability to look into the past and the future can be enticing, we should never look too far. It is like an undertow. Witches can end up stuck between the layers of realities, not knowing whether they are alive or dead, or where they are. It's a terrible fate for anyone. Yah taught me to be careful, which included learning to reign in the innate desire to know, and to recognize when something is more than I can handle. Not every bit of knowledge is safe. Or a better way to say it is, not every piece of knowledge is safe in everyone's hands. Even those with the best intentions.

Fifth, magic is a choice. A witch can, like Yah, decide at any point in her life to temper her magic or extinguish it altogether. It's easy to forget sometimes, having it be constantly available, that you can turn it off.

So why am I telling you, a stranger, my life story? I need your help, and I hear people are more willing to help if they know you. While I can use magic to make you drive me to San Francisco, I'd rather not. One, it would be extremely exhausting for me, and two, it won't be pleasant for you. My problem, a serious one, is my grandmother is missing. I don't know where she went. I don't know why. All I know is that she was not in her bed when I woke up.

Her behavior has been strange in the last few weeks before her disappearance. She would forget where she was, our names, even her own name. There was a word she would repeat over and over in her sleep, but I don't know what it means. *Chin-tha. Chin-tha. Chin-*

*tha*. The doctor said her memory had collapsed in on itself. But I don't believe it. I could still see magic in her—a part of her like the color of her eyes and her mountain of white hair. She's there. My fear is that she's trapped somewhere in that in-between place she had warned me about. I need to get her out before I lose her forever.

There's a witch in San Francisco who may be able to give me some answers. I can feel it—her magic. So, that's why I need you to get me there. If it makes you feel better, think of me as the east coast man, traveling across hundreds of miles for a dream. I'm sorry if this ruins your day. Like I said, I need your help.

# Love me, Tender

San Francisco, U.S.A., 1998

Violet stared at the empty spot in front of her neighbor's door. The longer she looked at it, the eerier it made her feel. It was as if it were a black hole where things disappeared into and never returned. That was the problem with routine.

Ever since she moved into the Fair Rosamund, a dilapidated, bug-infested, pay-by-the-week-cigarette-smoke-stewed hotel in the heart of the Tenderloin district, that spot had never been unoccupied. There, in the cul-de-sac adjacent to the elevator and the stairs, was where Kezia, the resident fortune teller, dispensed her macabre warnings to all the inhabitants of the fourth floor on their way to their disposable jobs.

"Step out of the building with your right foot or misfortune will befall you," she would cheerfully say, or something just as superstitious and grim.

To the fourth floor residents of the Fair Rosamund, the fortune teller's daily warnings, doled out with the tenderness of a mother's kiss, were the only constant in their lives. No morning was complete without them, especially this one.

Violet needed her. She had the old dream again last night—the one that had been haunting her, trailing her like a malevolent spirit since childhood. She thought she had left it behind in the hopeless Iowa town of her birth.

The memory of it surfaced. The claustrophobic feeling of being squeezed from all sides. The sound of disembodied breathing in her ears. The image of shadows broken by a stream of orange light. The sour smell of sweat. The rusty scent of blood. Her blood. Violet fought it off, furiously building a brick wall to cage it for the time being.

She looked at her watch. Seven o'clock.

*Where's Miss Kezia?*

Without her, the gray hallway looked drab and desolate. Dripping from head-to-toe in what she coined 'glorious gypsy,' Kezia was a carnival of ocular and auditory overstimulation. She wore mismatched layers of long flowy skirts and colorful billowy blouses that overwhelmed her petite frame. In her curly crimson hair was a headdress made of old coins and around both wrists and ankles were bracelets with bells that jingled whenever she moved.

Her table, covered with cloths of diverse origins in various states of decay, was as brightly dressed as she. On days the neighborhood florist who serviced the corporate hotels in Union Square was in a giving mood, it would be adorned with a fancy, albeit slightly wilted, flower arrangement as high as the ceiling.

Kezia told Violet the spot was perfect for what she needed it to be. As she shuffled her stack of age-stained tarot cards, she could see every fourth floor residents' comings and goings, feeling their energy. Many suspected she had threatened black magic on the last superintendent to get the choice location. But according to Kezia, she was beautiful in her twenties, when she first moved to the city, and before she had lost half her teeth. So perhaps it was not black magic but her feminine charms that did the last super in.

Violet knocked on the fortune teller's door.

"Miss Kezia. It's Violet. I have donuts, you want one?"

There was no answer, no sound from behind the peeling forest green door. The fortune teller was not the type to decline sweets, especially when free. Violet jiggled the door handle. It was locked. She wondered whom she could ask the whereabouts of the missing woman.

Kezia had her regulars. The hopeless romantics. The down-on-their-luck. The drunk-and-high. Some of her best customers were the trans hookers from the corner of Geary and Larkin. As long as they could pay her, the fortune teller did not care which body parts they had or did not have. But Violet could not predict when they would come.

Kezia's clientele was a fickle bunch. They could not help their nature, the old woman said. The hopeless romantics could fall in love and move out or give up and move out. The down-on-their-luck would not always be that way. The drunk-and-high were perpetually chasing the haze. The only ones she was able to consistently rely on were the prostitutes—at least those who did not fall into the drunk-and-high category. They always had cash.

Kezia had other clients too. Her regulars were not enough to sustain the ever-growing cost of living in bustling San Francisco, which in the late nineties was experiencing a new gold rush of the tech kind. Like a smart investor, she knew the beauty of diversification and was always soliciting new clients.

"You want your fortune read today?" Kezia would ask anyone as they walked past.

If the person looked especially downtrodden that day, she would offer to cleanse their aura.

Wednesdays were usually her best days, she told Violet. It was when people were sick of their dead-end, low-paying jobs and needed to be reminded the end of the week was within grasp. For the fortune reading, she would lay down the deck of tarot cards and allow three to be picked from the bunch. Then she would decipher them like ancient runes—one for the present, one for the past, and one for the future. For the aura cleansing, she would light up a bundle of sage, which would replace the reek of disinfectant in the hall, making it smell like a temple.

Kezia did not always take money. She knew the demographics of the Fair Rosamund were not the kind to always have it. If someone was walking by with a particularly delicious-smelling takeout, she might offer to do a reading in exchange for the contents. Sometimes she would even trade her services for kitchen duty. That was how Violet got her first reading.

Kezia, like many cash-strapped residents of the Fair Rosamund, paid for a part of her rent by working the small kitchen next to the lobby. No one ate there except the young international students who were renting rooms while studying English at the language school down the street. The food was subpar at best, but no foreign students stayed long enough to care. Even if they did, there was no point in complaining. The long-time veterans of the hotel ran the kitchen and they did not give a rat's ass what anyone thought of their cooking. Violet decided she would start there.

She took the elevator. The lighting in the windowless stairwell was unpredictable and she did not want to trip on the occasional druggie too impatient to wait for the privacy of their room. The metal box smelled strongly of disinfectant and, beneath that, the sickeningly sweet scent of vomit. Violet pushed the yellowed button for the lobby. The sign posted next to the button panel stated its last inspection was four years ago in 1994. At least there were only five floors to the building if ever the elevator decided to misbehave.

*Could one die by falling five floors in an elevator?*

Alec was sitting at the front desk. From his bleary eyes, she could tell he had worked the night shift.

"Have you seen Miss Kezia?" she asked.

"No," said Alec, his face scrunched up like a ball of yesterday's newspaper.

Violet noticed a scarlet line that ran from his ear to lips—a sign he had spent a better part of his shift sleeping.

"Useless," she mumbled under her breath and walked toward the dining room.

In the vast dimly lit space lined by foot-scraped carpet and age-faded wallpaper was a young couple—Japanese students judging from their designer hair and clothes. They were the only ones sitting in the room, wordlessly wolfing down their breakfast of scrambled eggs, bacon, and pancakes. The only sound was the high-pitched clacking of their utensils against plates like Morse code. *Send help, this place is shit.*

She pushed through the double doors into the kitchen and found Brad, her neighbor in room 438. He was standing in the middle of the room in a pose reminiscent of *Discobolus*, an ancient Greek statue of a man throwing a discus, which in his case was a round metal cookie sheet. Unlike the naked statue, he wore a white apron on top of red pajamas. From where she stood, she could not tell whether the print was of horses or elephants.

When he saw her he straightened as if, with her presence, she had lifted the spell that had turned him to stone. He ran one hand through his disheveled hair.

"Hey Violet! What's up buttercup?" he greeted, a bright smile decorating his boyishly handsome face.

Violet's heart used to flutter at the mere thought of his smile. When she first moved in, he helped her carry boxes into her room and showed her the ins and outs of the hotel. He was her knight in shining armor in those first few days. Then she heard a rumor of what he did for money—which was later substantiated by the inappropriate noises that came through their shared wall at random hours—and her admiration had dissipated. She remained civil nonetheless. Even if she did not love her neighbor, she figured she should at least tolerate him.

"Have you seen Miss Kezia?" she asked. "I knocked on her door but she didn't answer."

"No, but I started at six. Maybe she just went out. Did you ask Alec?"

"He fell asleep."

"Bastard."

"I'm worried," said Violet.

Her anxiety over the missing fortune teller was undoubtedly premature. For all she knew Kezia could just be having a nice breakfast in a cafe with an old friend. But her feelings were telling her that something strange had transpired, and if there was one thing she had learned from Kezia, it was to believe in her feelings.

Violet knew what she had to do next, but she did not want to do it. Her desperation must have shown on her face because a look of understanding began to unfold on Brad's. She could tell from his expression that he felt the same.

"Let me talk to Alec," he said, finally.

They both walked out of the kitchen into the lobby, past the silent foreign couple who were now staring into their empty plates as if surprised by their ability to consume subpar food. Once they arrived at Alec's desk, Brad leaned on the fake wood partition separating them. He composed his countenance into one he thought was his most intimidating. But, with his silly pajamas, he was nowhere near frightening. Violet appreciated the gesture nonetheless.

"Hey, butthead, Miss Kezia's not answering her door. You're gonna have to call Mister Will," said Brad.

"No way!" Alec said.

"You fell asleep on the job," Brad said with a threatening undertone.

"No, I didn't!"

Violet rolled her eyes. "The evidence is on your face."

Alec frantically tried to look at his reflection on the computer screen in front of him.

"So either you call him or we'll call him and mention you sleeping," said Brad.

Alec shuddered. His nervousness had nothing to do with Brad. Mister Will, the superintendent, was a six-foot-four black man with the bearing of a combat-hardened ex-marine and hands big enough to crush a watermelon—or a human skull. He was not someone the residents went to for frivolous things. Everyone, even the newest international students, knew you only call Mister Will with emergencies. The story was, the body of the last person who had annoyed him with a trivial request was buried inside the walls of the Fair Rosamund. No one could verify it of course, but Mister Will never tried to dispute the rumor either.

Alec, face bleached of color, dialed the number to the super's room.

"Hello, Mister Will. This is Alec from the front desk."

The voice on the other side said something that made Alec's face turned a paler shade of pale.

"Yes, sir, I know what time it is. But uh—Violet and Brad from the fourth floor are here with me. They—uh—they said Miss Kezia is not answering her door. They seem worried. Can you please check? Uh—sir."

"I'm going back up to wait for him," said Violet.

"I'll go with you," Brad said.

"What about the kitchen?"

"It's fine." He turned to Alec. "Call my room if someone wants food."

"Whatever," Alec said.

Violet knew he would do as Brad asked. You do not get on the bad side of a cook. There are too many sharp tools at their disposal.

While they were standing next to each other in the elevator, she stole a closer look at the pattern on Brad's red pajamas. The animals were actually toy trucks. She really should get her eyes checked—if only she could afford it.

He yawned.

"Late night?" Violet asked. She knew it was. She heard through their wall.

"A bit. The early shift in the kitchen didn't help. And after this I have a job at the art school," he said.

Many who lived at the Fair Rosamund had multiple odd jobs. They had to. It was a matter of surviving the city.

"What job at the art school?" she asked.

His faced colored. "It's stupid. Easy money, but stupid."

"Can't be worse than scraping gum off sidewalks." That was one of her jobs.

Or as morally crippled as his other job, selling homemade pornographic videotapes. She had seen the women he brought in to star in them. Most looked as if they were on spring break in Cancun. She doubted if any of them knew they were actresses in his productions. The only consolation was he only sold the tapes to tourists from other countries. At least that was what people said.

"I just have to stand still and let the students sketch me." Brad sighed. "Naked."

Violet let out an unintended guffaw.

Brad's face turned a shade of ruby. "I told you it was stupid."

*That explains the Discobolus pose.*

"Nah. It's actually kinda cool. Odd. But cool," she said as they stepped out of the elevator.

Mister Will arrived at Kezia's door wearing a gray sweat suit. His normally clean-shaven head was shadowy from a two-day growth and his eyes were bloodshot. He looked as if he also had a late night.

"Hello," they said. The super acknowledged them with a nod.

Mister Will's giant fist knocked on the door, rattling it like a five on the Richter scale.

"Miss Kezia, it's Will. Please open."

No answer. He took off the keychain from around his neck and unlocked the door with the skeleton key. It swung open with a creak to reveal a dark room empty of its inhabitant.

The only window was covered by thick, blood-red curtains. Mister Will flicked the light switch and the room lit up like a plush jinni lair. Vibrant fabrics draped the walls. Glittering glass bottles like jewels decorated the window sill and dressing table. Kezia's bed, buried under a luxuriant quantity of Indian textiles, was neatly made as if she had not slept in it. The card table, which Violet had helped bring in last night, sat in the corner where they had placed it.

"Anything missing?" asked Mister Will.

Violet looked around the room. Kezia did not have any valuables worth stealing. No electronics. No jewelry. No drugs. The glass bottles were of essential oils she used in her healing ceremonies.

Violet's eyes came to rest on the bedside table. Blood froze solid in her digits.

"Her deck of tarot cards. She usually keeps it next to her when she sleeps. It's not there."

*Where's Miss Kezia?*

"We need to find her," she said, her voice quivering. A feeling of dread filled her.

"There's nothing you can do now. Go to work," Mister Will said. "I'll ask around."

\* \* \*

After making the necessary calls to inquire about the missing fortune teller, Will settled back on his chair. It was a proper office chair with an arch back support and adjustable armrests, and fairly new. He had bought it at the Salvation Army. Most everything he owned was from there or some other network of thrift stores and charity shops. In its past life it must have belonged to a start-up tech company whose dreams had come to naught. As many overnight successes as there were, there were more failures. Such was the way life worked in the city.

He stared unblinkingly at the black screen of the laptop he had bought with a month's salary. He blamed Kezia for this extravagant purchase. She told him he would need it to fulfill his destiny.

"To do what?" he had asked then.

"To play God," the fortune teller had said. "You've been wanting to do it. It's been calling out to you. You're meant for this path."

Since he bought the expensive machine he had been prolific, writing thousands of words a day. The story seemed to have materialized out of thin air with characters fully formed—one birth of Venus after another. He took inspiration from his richly woven life. People he encountered became gargoyles, dragons, and knights; ordinary interactions became battle scenes and journeys into danger; illogical rants heard on the streets chanted in the fog of drugs became spells.

But now something was different. He could feel it. Something dark

69

and dense was growing inside, as if the black pit of the screen had somehow burrowed its way in.

It did not help that he was exhausted. It was the dream. In it, his walls were infested with little people the size of his thumb with bodies thickly covered from head to feet with fine hair as dark and glittery as black sand and eyes that blazed the color of the sun. There was a whole village of them. They were dancing around a bonfire to music he could not hear. In the burning pyre was something Will knew was precious—white and hard like a cloudy diamond—but he was powerless to stop it from turning into ashes.

*What was it?*

The thought of not knowing made him want to weep. It was the fortune teller's fault for opening his third eye and unleashing his vulnerability. A writer was supposed to milk all the beauty and the ugliness from the udder of the world and drink it in a cup, she had said. That was the necessary hazard of the profession. Before she read his fortune, which he had avoided for years, he never dared think of his life as more than the Fair Rosamund. Now he had travelled too far to turn back. He had dared to dream.

* * *

That night, Violet came back from her job cracking crabs at the Wharf for tourists, fingers wrinkled and raw, to a meeting being held in the dining room. It seemed the news of Kezia's disappearance had spread swiftly through the small community of the Fair Rosamund, like a particularly infectious venereal disease. The fact that the meeting was organized by the flighty residents of the hotel was a feat worth noting.

The group stood in a loose circle, swapping theories. The disappearance of Kezia was akin to having the entire building of the Fair Rosamund vanish without a trace overnight. Violet found a spot near the pitiful salad bar where the same two Japanese students from breakfast were assembling wilted edible art on their plates. Next to her was Brad, no longer wearing his red pajamas, now in a respectable pair of dirty jeans and a black t-shirt.

"Was a police report filed?" asked Mira, a young art student in room 412.

"Yes," said Mister Will's deep voice.

Everyone shifted their attention in his direction. He was sitting alone at one of the tables, staring at his interlaced large hands.

"Oh, that's great!" Mira said, her voice artificially chirpy. She was surprised to get a response from the taciturn super.

"I think we should make a missing person flyer and post it all over the city," said Violet.

"Great idea!" Brad said. "I know a guy with a copy machine. Do you have a photo of her we can use?"

Violet shook her head.

"Does anybody?"

No one at the meeting had—not even Marsha, the photographer wannabe in 529.

"Mira, can you draw her picture?" asked Starr, one of Kezia's transvestite clients.

She was wearing a Farrah Fawcett blonde wig and a matching sparkly mini dress to draw attention away from the nose that looked similar to her Beatle namesake. Under her eyes was hastily wiped tear-dissolved mascara. She must have recently found out about the missing fortune teller, Violet thought.

"I'm a conceptual artist," Mira said, which to Violet meant she did not know how to draw.

"But how about this," said the artist. "I'll come up with words to describe Miss Kezia. Not boring like what the cops use in a police report. Ones that, like, fit her essence. You know, her true self."

Everyone stared at her.

"And since Brad has a camera, we'll, like, tape everyone saying these words," Mira added, more excited by the minute. "It'll be like poetry. You know. A chant. It'll speak to the souls of everyone living in San

Francisco. And we can juxtapose the words with, like, images from the streets. And it'll be—transcendental."

Violet could not help but roll her eyes.

"Girl, by the time we find Miss Kezia that way, she be dead," Starr said.

"And how are you gonna get anyone to see it? Public access television?" asked Violet.

A blank look crossed Mira's face. An artist was not supposed to have to worry about such mundane things.

"I used to draw," said Brad. "I don't know if I'm any good now. But I'll give it a try."

Everyone agreed to let him try.

"What we goin' say on the flyer?" asked Starr.

It was a simple question packed with complexity. Even though the fortune teller was known by everyone, she was an enigmatic figure. It was mainly by her own design. On the subject of her origin, there were contradicting stories. To some, she said she was from Romania, even though she could not speak Romanian. To others, she said Ireland was her home, but her accent sounded more like a New Yorker than anything else.

Even her age was a mystery. One could assume she was between fifty and sixty if they added the age she came to the city (that she may or may not have lied about) with the speculated number of years she had been living at the hotel (which not even Mister Will had a record of). Contributing to the difficulty was her face. Her cheeks partially sank in due to her lack of teeth while her skin was still supple from her religious application of coconut oil. She was the fossil that refused to be carbon-dated.

She did not have any family to verify her life story either. The tale she supplied had her as an orphan separated from her siblings during the war, although she would not confirm which war or which country. When pressed, she would call it something generic like the Great War or the Ten Year Conflict.

There were only three things everyone who knew her could agree on:

1) She had been at the Fair Rosamund a long time.

2) She was a mostly accurate fortune teller.

3) She was loved by all.

So, the topic of her description was much-debated.

*Between four-eleven and five-foot-two. It's hard to tell, she's always sitting.*

*Single white female. You sure she's not secretly married?*

*A hundred, maybe a hundred and twenty pounds. She wears a lot of clothes.*

*Bottle-dyed red hair. Curly.*

*Blue eyes. No, they're green. No, they're hazel. The lighting in the hallway sucks.*

*Accompanied by a jingling like Santa's sleigh.*

*Missing some teeth.*

*Smells of sage. And sometimes patchouli.*

*An air of mystery.*

*Fortune Teller Extraordinaire.*

*Contact Will at the Fair Rosamund.*

"Five-O" a voice yelled from the lobby.

Before Violet could decide what to do, everyone scattered and disappeared into their respective holes like mice. Mister Will got up from his seat and came to stand next to her.

"They're here to talk to us," he said.

Violet regretted not having left. Although she knew she had nothing to be afraid of, the anxiety the hotel residents had around the authorities was contagious.

Two police officers entered the dining room and introduced themselves. The unsmiling blonde, who looked as if she could beat any man to a pulp, was Officer Pattinson. Her partner, a stout Hispanic man with a jovial face, was Officer Valdez. By this point, only four people were left: Violet, Mister Will, Brad (surprisingly), and Anne, the ex-junkie from the second floor who claimed the fortune teller had cured her.

"So, you're the one who saw Kezia last?" Officer Pattinson asked.

"Yes. My room is next to hers," said Violet.

"And your name?"

"Violet Corbet." She pronounced her last name with a 't'.

"What was she doing?"

"She was moving her table back into her room and I helped."

"What was the table for?"

"Her job. She's a fortune teller. Her—uh—office is in front of her door."

"Did she seem *different* to you?"

Violet did not know how to answer. Did the policewoman mean different as in strange or unlike her usual self?

"Ma'am?"

"Sorry, I was trying to recall," said Violet. "I mean she's always been an odd person. But she's friendly and sweet. She asks me all the time how I'm doing and if I like the city. I haven't been here that long, so I can't tell you how different she was from her normal self, but she was just as chatty as usual."

"Did you hear anything strange from her room that night?"

Violet debated whether she should tell the officer the noise from Brad's extracurricular activity on the other side of the wall had made it impossible for her to hear anything else. She decided against it.

"No."

"When did you realize she was gone?" Officer Pattinson asked.

"This morning. She wasn't in front of her room and I thought it odd because she's usually the first one up. I knocked to see if she wanted breakfast, but she didn't answer."

"Was the door locked?"

Violet nodded. "We had to ask Mister Will to open it so we could check on her."

"And was anything taken from her room?"

"I only noticed her tarot cards gone. She always has them with her though."

Officer Pattinson turned to the super. "Did the front desk person see her leave?"

"He said he didn't," said Mister Will.

"Does she have any enemies? Anybody who dislikes her."

"No."

"Have you tried calling her emergency contact?"

"She doesn't have one listed."

"She doesn't have family?"

"We're her family," Mister Will said. "Everyone who lives here."

The policewoman closed her little black bound notebook.

"Well, at this point, we don't have much to go by. A missing person's case can be open for years. She's an adult of sound mind, and it's within her rights to go anywhere she chooses."

"But what if she didn't choose it?" asked Brad. "What if she was taken?"

"No one saw her leave her room or with a stranger. No one heard any unusual noises. There's nothing to go by."

"What about the evil spirits?" asked Anne.

"Excuse me?" Officer Pattinson said.

"Miss Kezia told me about them the other day—these little creatures that live inside walls. They can take you to their world. What if they kidnapped her and took her away?"

The policewoman turned to Mister Will, ignoring Anne, and gave him her card. "Call me if you have anything else to report."

"Thanks for coming, officers," Mister Will said. He patted Officer Valdez's back. "Manny."

"No problem, man," said Officer Valdez.

After both police officers left, all eyes were on Anne.

"Why did you have to tell her that? Now she's gonna think Miss Kezia is crazy," said Brad.

"She never told you guys about the evil spirits in the walls?" asked Anne.

"No," said Violet and Brad at once.

"And you, Mister Will?"

"It doesn't matter. Got nothing to do with her being missing," said the super before turning about face and walking away.

\* \* \*

Will almost tripped on the loose strings on the threadbare carpet as he rushed to his room. He kept his eyes fixed straight ahead, not daring to look at the loiterers hanging out in the hallway as he passed. They must not see the fear in his eyes. He could not afford to lose the façade—a hardened persona he needed to run a hotel where its wealthy owners refused to spend an extra dime on upkeep.

He unlocked the door with shaky hands as an unending line of questions raced through his mind like stinging ants toward prey. How did Miss Kezia know about the little wall creatures from his dream? Did she steal them out of him with witchcraft? Why did she tell Anne? Was it to humiliate him? What else did she say? Who else did she tell?

He entered the room and shut the door with a loud bang. He leaned against it, his breath coming up short and quick from shame. The worst would be if the fortune teller had divulged the details of their sessions to everyone. His stomach churned at the thought of his private life airdrying in full view—the residents of the Fair Rosamund knowing about his aspirations and fears.

*But she wouldn't.* Kezia had never once betrayed her clients. That was why he trusted her. Then he realized he only dreamed about the creatures last night, the same night she went missing. She could not have known. He began to feel better at the thought.

There was logic to this, he reasoned. The residents of the Fair Rosamund were prone to gossip and tall tales. It did not help that the hotel, with its peeling corridors and dripping faucets, was a perfect backdrop for paranormal stories. The original building was erected in the late 1800's. It was partially destroyed in the infamous seven-point-nine magnitude earthquake of 1906 and the ensuing fire that burned for days. A new building was later constructed around it. Encased in the new structure were the remains of the original old brick walls. He had seen them. So it was not difficult to imagine dark fairytales emerging from the Fair Rosamund—and somehow, they had seeped into his dream. But try as he might, he could not recall the time he had heard the story about the little wall creatures.

Maybe it had come from one of the books he read, he thought. There were enough of them in the crammed bookcase that stood floor to ceiling against a wall in his room. History of the Bay Area stretched far back with human habitation dating to 3,000 BC. Native Americans had settled in the region for its plentiful resources, from the bay and the surrounding forests, before the Spaniards found it in 1769. The bones of a five-thousand-year-old woman were found during excavations done while the city was developing the BART station at the Civic Center. Maybe the creatures from his dream were from a Native American mythology, and not the same ones Kezia told Anne about. He sighed. His overactive imagination had once again gotten the better of him.

\* \* \*

Violet lifted the creaky window pane to let the cool night air in. Her room faced the alley and she could hear Starr's voice from below, hustling. It looked like she was back at work despite her distraught state. Starr was one of Kezia's best customers—hardworking and dependable, desperately trying to claw her way out of the gutter that was her life. Violet wondered what Starr and Kezia talked about in their sessions and what advice the fortune teller gave her.

She leaned on the headboard and opened a book to the page she had marked with the sleeping cat bookmark she got from Chinatown. She had been trying to finish it for a month. The writer's prose was a confusingly complex arrangement of words, apparently strung together for their beauty and not for the ease of reading. But she felt that if she could finish the book something would change and her life would be better. It was Kezia's idea.

The fortune teller told Violet that her time at the Fair Rosamund was temporary. She was the wind passing through, soon to move on to another place, another country. One day, she would leave the embrace of this hotel and its people and enter a world filled with the traps and deceptions of humanity, where motivations were opaque, and a smile was a veil. But before that, she would need to arm herself with knowledge from books written by wise sages who understood the complexity of the world and its people. Violet's compass, the one she brought with her to this place, was broken. *Fix it,* Kezia said. That was the only way she would survive—and survive she would.

Violet stared at the first sentence on the page—the words two-stepping as if they were at a honky-tonk. She was too distracted to read, but she pushed through, aligning each word neatly next to each other like soldiers standing in a line. She did not know how much time had passed when she heard a knock on the door.

*Miss Kezia?!*

"Coming!" she jumped off the bed.

She yanked open the door. There was no one there. She stuck her head out and looked down the long hallway. It was empty. The first thing she felt was anger. Someone was playing a trick on her at the most inappropriate, thoughtless time. Then she felt a chill—it sent a shiver up her spine, making the hair on the back of her neck stand up.

She slammed the door shut and ran back to her bed. Once her heart slowed, she decided it was the druggies from 415—the two young men who, when high, would dare each other to perform stupid stunts that bordered on dangerous. They had probably run out of ideas to experiment with on each other and had moved on to her. She wanted to scream but settled on staring at the amoeba-shaped brown stain on the ceiling instead.

Another series of knocks. She bolted upright. For one moment she wondered if she should jump out the window and run down the fire escape to the safety of Starr.

"Violet," Brad's voice said from the other side.

She sprung off the bed and opened the door.

"Was it you?" Her voice was harsher than she had intended.

"Uh—what? I just heard a loud bang from your room and wanted to see if you were okay."

"Oh." She unraveled her arms from her chest. "I'm fine."

"What was that about?"

"Someone knocked on my door earlier, but when I opened it, no one was there."

Brad's eyebrows knotted. "Probably some asshole wanting to scare a girl."

Violet noticed a piece of paper in his hand.

"What's that?" she asked.

"It's a sketch of Miss Kezia."

"Can I see?"

"It's not done." He handed it to her, his face was a mixture of apprehension and shyness, neither of which she had seen on him before.

Violet was surprised by the caliber of the details on the fortune teller's face, especially around her eyes.

"It's really good," she said.

Brad's face lit up. "You think so?"

"Everyone will know it's her for sure. Do you want help adding the descriptions?"

"Yeah. I can't remember what we ended up with."

"We can work at my desk," she said. She did not trust Brad's booby-trapped room.

They decided on the best descriptions of the fortune teller and added Mister Will's contact information. They were good at working around each other and Violet was amazed how comfortable she felt in Brad's presence.

"What do you think happened to her?" he asked. His eyes were on the drawing as his hands added more shadows under Kezia's cheekbones.

"I don't know. I've heard of old people who lose their memory and can't remember their way home. Maybe she walked out in the middle of the night and just—forgot."

"She doesn't seem the type. She knows everything that goes on in the building."

"Sometimes it can happen quickly. There was an old widower from my town who was found dead in the snow one Christmas morning. He lived alone after his wife passed. His kids all live in other states. By the time someone saw him, wild animals had eaten half his face."

Her mother had told this story so many times, burying it like a seed of guilt to keep her from leaving their dead-end town. Violet regretted that she had let it work for as long as it did.

Brad shuddered. "So you think she's just out there—wandering the streets?"

"I hope not. At least it's summer. And California."

Then Violet heard it. A noise like someone banging their headboard against the wall. It was coming from next door. Brad's room. The hair on her arms stood up.

"Did you hear that?" Violet whispered.

"What?"

"That sound. Do you have somebody in your room?"

"No."

He reached over to her window and closed it, shutting out the distractions from the streets. The sound came again. Deep and deliberate. *Thunk. Thunk. Thunk.*

"That's not coming from my room," he said.

They looked at each other. Violet's room only had two neighbors.

\* \* \*

Will's hollow reflection taunted him from the black mirror of the ex-

80

pensive machine, laughing at his wordlessness—an affliction—erectile dysfunction of the brain.

*Serves you right, you idiot.*

His story, a half-alive being, clawed at his mind, gnawing on the white tissue of his frontal lobes. There was a pang in his stomach—an acute, obsessive desire to write so he could release his characters—his people—from their bondage. But he could not. It was as if the entire world he had created was caged behind an impenetrable granite wall. No one could get out. Not the giantess of the blue forest. Not the ninety-eight-armed goddess of the underworld. Not even the powerful evil wizard, the most wicked being in his world.

Will's head pounded. He closed his eyes and massaged his temples. The dark gray void behind his lids soothed him and he decided to stay there. In its emptiness he could hear the rhythmic beating of his heart. *Thm. Thm. Thm. Thm.* It called out to the missing fortune teller.

*Where's Miss Kezia?*

He wondered if she was safe. Was she hungry? Cold? Afraid? He imagined her petite body trembling in the dark, the jingling of her bracelets the only sound in the still air.

The gray behind his lids glowed and slowly changed to orange. The blurry shade became the flames of the bonfire and the shadows around it transformed to the thumb-sized people dancing. The image grew until it overwhelmed his vision.

He felt a pull at his center as if someone had yanked his belly button, and he found himself next to the creatures in the circle. The freezing wind blew from the bonfire like a polar vortex from the north, yet he was not cold. Around him the coal-colored creatures danced, legs and arms swaying like the branches of a willow tree. They wore nothing but the thick hair on their skin that glistened in the flickering light like crushed dark stars. The outline of their bodies was surrounded by an aura like the sun's corona. They reminded him of a total solar eclipse—in humanoid form. His heart beat the devil's tattoo in his chest.

One of the creatures noticed him. It stared at him with its sun-colored eyes, its hairy lips moving, saying something. *What did it say?*

He tilted his head to one side to focus on the sound. *Let me hear.* It was as if a button had been pushed. His ears were filled at once with the music—the drumming, the strumming, the humming—an alien tune he had never before heard.

*Dance,* the creature said. *Dance with us.* It was less a request than an order. Will knew he did not have any option but to follow. So he did. As he mimicked their steps, his arms flailing above his head, he followed their gaze. They were all staring into the fire and at the large white object burning in it. It looked like an organically shaped four-legged table carved out of smooth marble. In and of itself, the table did not look threatening, yet a fear so raw and primal clutched at his heart.

Suddenly the music stopped. The thumb people stood still like mannequins. All eyes were on him—red and laser-like—burning his skin with the intensity of the desert sun. They asked him a wordless question that aroused a deep craving, a ravenous desire.

*Yes. Yes. Please give it to me,* he answered.

*In return we want one thing,* they said. *One little thing.*

*Anything.*

They surrounded him like ants to a crumb. Each reached out a finger to touch a spot on his bare skin. He felt an electric current running through him, as if a life force—an unearthly energy—had been transferred into his body. Something solid but transparent slithered over his skin, coiling around his arms and legs, binding him. Before he could scream, he felt a sharp, piercing pain on his lips. They were being sewn shut.

The pounding on the door startled him. Will sat up and rubbed his eyes. He glanced at his watch. No one had ever bothered him in his off hours before. He sighed and composed his face to the hardened mask of the unsympathetic superintendent.

At the door was the girl, Violet. With hair the color of corn silk and eyes sad like a wheat field after harvest, he had modeled a character after her—a heroine in search of an elixir to bring back her lost childhood. She was, at the moment, trapped behind the rock wall like everyone else, and Will needed to help her find a way out.

"Mister Will, you have to come!" Violet said. Her eyes looked as if she had just been chased by a pack of crazed trolls.

He ran after her and came to Kezia's door. Brad was waiting there, guarding it. He looked as though he was ready to jump on a warhorse and ride into battle.

"We heard a sound coming from her room. We knocked but no one answered," Brad said.

"What kind of sound?" Will asked.

"Like something hard banging against the wall," said Violet. "I heard the same sound last night. But louder and more urgent. I thought it came from Brad's side. But he just told me he didn't even get home 'til one."

Will unlocked the door and clicked on the light. Kezia's room was just as he had seen it that morning. He entered, Violet and Brad following behind him. Once inside, their eyes scanned every corner of the odd shaped room.

"No one's here. Are you sure you heard something?" Will asked.

"I swear," Violet said.

"We wouldn't have bothered you if we weren't sure," said Brad.

Will believed them.

"Violet, tell him what happened earlier," added Brad.

The girl looked uncomfortable. "It's probably not related."

"Tell me anyways," said Will.

"Someone knocked on my door. I thought it was Miss Kezia, so I ran to open it. There was no one there. I looked down the hall, but it was empty. I didn't hear anyone's door close or any footsteps on the stairs either."

Violet shivered, and Will felt a cold wave running through him. After all the years he had been at the Fair Rosamund, he had come to know the place intimately—her every secret, every flaw. Yet, he had never been afraid of her. He decided he would not start now.

"Miss Kezia!" he yelled. "If you're here, let us know."

Brad took an unconscious step in front of Violet, shielding her.

*Has the stable boy decided to become a knight?* Will wondered. *About time.*

Violet headed to the closet and opened it.

"Miss Kezia!" she yelled into the dark space.

A loud thump echoed through the room and the three froze like meerkats in the Serengeti under the shadow of a hawk.

"That's the sound," Violet whispered.

"It came from the walls," said Brad.

"She's trapped inside it! She must be," Violet said, her eyes watering.

Something in Will clicked, coming together like puzzle pieces. There was no time to question, to reason, to doubt. Without another word, he ran down the hall to the utility room. As he rummaged for what he needed, he heard movement behind him.

"What are you doing?" Violet asked.

Will looked over his shoulder and saw her and Brad, their faces bewildered.

He answered them by handing each a hammer and a flashlight. A look of understanding dawned on the two. They nodded in agreement.

The three walked back into the room, laden with heavy tools and hearts. Will closed the door and bolted it. *Keep the lookie-loos out.*

"Which wall?" Brad asked.

"Doesn't matter," Will answered. They all had to be opened.

He walked to a wall, the one closest to Kezia's bed, and swung the hammer. The thin drywall gave in as white chalk from its innards fell onto the grubby carpeted floor. He hit again, harder this time, and struck the brick wall. The aged bricks crumbled, leaving a gaping hole. The smell of stale air and mildew wafted out from the other side. He stuck his face against the wall and saw nothing but an empty gap. He lifted his hammer again and repeated the process.

Behind him, Brad was working on the shared wall between this room and Violet's. The girl was in the closet, the place she had yelled for Kezia. The sounds of smashing and crashing reverberated through the room. Soon, the residents of the Fair Rosamund would come out of their holes to sniff the air for danger, Will knew. Then he would deal with it. But at this moment he must take down the walls.

"Mister Will! Brad!" he heard Violet yell.

* * *

Violet stared into the dark corridor. As wide as an average person and as long as the building, it ran straight like an underground train tunnel. With brick walls on either side and weathered gray wood floors, the passageway looked as if it had been swallowed by the Fair Rosamund and was in the process of being digested.

"What's this place?" Violet asked.

"Must be part of the original building. They just built around it after the fire," Mister Will said.

Violet watched as the super shifted his broad body sideways and squeezed through, his shirt scraping the chalky walls. The memory of the bad dream resurfaced. Her fear of it warred with her concern for the missing fortune teller. She shuddered at the thought of Kezia being buried alive in-between. She bit her lip, drawing blood. Her hand tightened around the flashlight, pressing the hard metal into her flesh to keep her grounded in reality. She took a step.

The creaky floor was covered with ancient layers of hardened dust. Bits of brick and mortar that had broken off the sides littered the path. With each crushing step, they disintegrated into powder, embedding their fine grains into the skin of the vulnerable old wood floors.

Brad was silent behind her. He had been quiet ever since they entered the dark passage. Violet wondered what he was thinking. She thought of the many times she had cursed through the wall over the ruckus she believed was from his deviant porn business. Did he even have a porn business? Who told her that rumor anyway? She could not remember.

Like Kezia, everyone knew Brad and he knew everyone. But unlike the fortune teller, he had a knack for rubbing some people the wrong way. He was one of the veterans of the hotel even though he was no more than a few years older than she. According to the rumor, which she now doubted, he was birthed here by a mother who traded her body for cash and smack. She left him when he was a teenager—the details were murky in regard to where she went. But he continued to live here, the Fair Rosamund being the only home he ever knew.

Violet wondered if Kezia had read his fortune too, and whether she also told him he would one day leave this place. Like her. Like the wind. Would he survive out there in the voracious jaws of the real world?

She realized then nothing and no one was as she believed them to be. In front of her was Mister Will, the frightening superintendent—the man whom everyone said was as cruel and heartless as the devil. Behind her was Brad, the porn king—the gigolo people said lured women into his deceptive den for his own gains. Each of them made up of layers of truths and lies solidified by perception. But in this moment, as she walked between these two men, she had never felt safer—not in the Iowa town that took her innocence, not in the unforgiving church that taught her to fear, not in her childhood house that held terrible secrets. The fortune teller was right—Violet's compass was broken. But she was fixing it. She was beginning to see.

Her foot slid on a different surface—something smooth. She looked down and shone the light on it. *Paper?*

"What is it?" Brad asked.

She lifted her foot. The image was of a skeleton sitting with its arms folded across its chest. She had seen it before.

"The death card," she said.

She slowly lowered herself onto her haunches in the cramped space and picked up the card. "It's one of Miss Kezia's tarot cards."

The thumping of her beating heart filled her ears. There was more than one possible reason for finding the card in the dark corridor in between walls inside the Fair Rosamund. But she could not think of one with a positive outcome.

She cast her light around the floor, looking for more signs the old woman was here.

"I think there's something ahead," said Mister Will.

The three banded closer together and stepped forward, shuffling like shackled prisoners, cautiously, as if underfoot was a minefield. Black thoughts swirled in Violet's head. She tried to focus instead on each footstep, as she did the words in a book, arranging them in neat lines one after another until they made sense.

Soon, they came to a space a little bigger than the room they had left. It was odd-shaped with no square corners, as if it was made up of the gaps and the left over from all the rooms on the fourth floor. The three spread out, shining their flashlights around the dark chamber. It was lined with crumbling bricks—a part of the original building. Kezia was not here.

Violet noticed a little tin box sitting in a hole cut out from the wall. It was orange and red, like flames painted against a dark night. She walked toward it and picked it up. It was light in her hand. She shook the tin and heard the rattling sound of something hard and small like marbles banging against each other. She pried open the rusted cover. What she saw inside made her legs give out from under her.

\* \* \*

Will heard a commotion followed by Brad's yelling.

The super turned and saw Violet sitting on the floor with Brad propping up her back, her face bleached of blood. He rushed to them.

"Violet! What's wrong?"

When he was close, the girl handed a small box to him without words.

"What is—" His voice disappeared into the darkness when he saw.

*Teeth!* Perfect specimens of glowing ivory. Except for one. On the molar, the biggest with four roots, was a trace of fresh blood glistening in the shadows.

*The white table burning in the bonfire. The coal creatures' object of obsession.*

A realization came—as if a veil had been lifted—as if the knowledge had been inside him all along. He remembered the dream. The wall people's offer. His agreement. The deal he did not know he had made and that he was bound to forever.

"I think they're Miss Kezia's," Violet said. "All the ones she lost."

"Why are they here?" Brad asked.

Will touched his lips—remembering the pain from the dream. He knew he could not tell anyone about the coal creatures. To do so would break the contract, the one sealed by the cold fire in a dream. *Kezia had paid the price for telling Anne about the evil spirits.*

"She's gone," he whispered, feeling his heart sinking at the words.

"What?! What do you mean?" Brad asked.

"There's fresh blood. She's gone," Will said.

"But where's her body? Where is she?!" Brad yelled.

*Burned in the fire.*

Will knew, the same way he now knew the ending of his book. It was the fortune teller's fate. As it was now his. He had made a deal with the coal creatures, just as Kezia did, for the return of words—the key to unlock the gate of his world. He needed to free the heroine and the knight, the giantess and the goddess, the dragons and the gargoyles. Without words, his words, they would be lost forever.

# Ghost Moon

New York City, U.S.A., 2018

"This was supposed to be the year I got a promotion!" Clementine screamed into the phone. "You said so."

Streaks of mascara painted parallel lines on her face, making her look as though she was ready for war.

"Then how do you explain what just happened?" Her voice sounded shrill in her ears, like her mother's when she was in manic mode.

She paused while listening to the voice on the other side of the line.

"Mercury retrograde? What's that supposed to mean?"

Her eyebrows knitted together. She brought her right hand to her lips and began to nibble at her finger nails.

"Hmm. Shadow period? That sounds awful. What do you recommend?"

She stared at the blue logo dancing on her computer monitor. Skydome. Pantone© 293. She had picked it. Psychologically, blue was supposed to evoke calm and trust. The color of stability and reliability.

The image bounced across the screen like a blue bunny. She always thought Blue Bunny would make a good capital name. No one would bomb a city called Blue Bunny. Blue Bunny, Iraq. She was being royally fucked by the color blue.

"Okay. Okay. Umm hmm. Today? Yeah, I can be there," she said, feeling as if she was being handed a life line.

A series of heavy knocks rapped against the door and Clementine jumped. She realized then she had been biting her nails. Such a bad habit.

"Just a minute!" she yelled at the door. Then she whispered into the phone, "I need to go. I'll see you tonight."

She unlocked the door. It was The Owl from HR. Everyone called her that behind her back. Clementine did not even know why. The woman looked nothing like the bird except for her tawny brown hair. Maybe it was her wise expression. Or her heart-shaped face.

The Owl took a step back when she saw Clementine. The HR Director cleared her throat in an attempt to be professional. You have to be professional when you have an office with a door.

"Are you ready?" The Owl said. Her voice was deep and melodious.

The Director of HR wondered whether she should tell Clementine about her mascara stained face. There was nothing in the company's manual about how to professionally handle someone else's embarrassment.

*The poor girl. She has no idea.* She decided she would tell her because it was a good thing to do. It was akin to telling someone they had spinach in their teeth or a post-it note stuck to their bum. Awkward, yet necessary.

"Before we leave, you may want to look in the mirror."

"What?"

"A mirror. Do you have one? Use the window. It's almost dark enough."

Clementine walked to the expanse of high quality one-inch sealed insulated glass. A year back, she read about a window falling out of the 27th floor of a financial district high rise, almost crushing a congregation of smokers. If the window had smashed just a few feet closer, it would have been the quickest death from smoking in the history of mankind. Would the Surgeon General put that on the warning labels?

Clementine wished for a cigarette. She deserved it after a day like today. But at ten dollars a pack, she would rather have a Starbucks coffee and a scone. She would never make it as a dedicated smoker, constantly wondering what better purchases she could make with the money.

Below, Broadway was packed. Tourists. Taxis. Terrorists. The trinity of nuisance in the life of a New Yorker. At least the terrorists were not a daily problem. At least not yet.

Against the maniacally blinking signs of musical shows, chain restaurants, and billboard advertisements, she saw the reflection of her face. Pale. Drawn. Defeated. The only color on it was the black streaks from her eyes that looked as if she had been crying a river of soot. For one moment she thought of leaving them on her face as a middle finger to the corporation. Like a nose ring or a facial tattoo.

She wondered if she should get a nose ring. A cute diamond one like Doria Ragland wore to the royal wedding. But, she thought, if the mother of the princess bride could pair it with an Oscar de la Renta dress, maybe it was not big enough of a fuck you to the establishment.

The Owl looked at her with a mixture of sympathy and disapproval. Clementine knew she was not being stoic and brave, not taking it like a grown professional woman. But she could not give a rat's ass. She was beyond caring. Not a day went by in her office when she did not hear "it's just business, it's not personal" coming from someone's mouth. She always hated that bullshit mantra of Ivy League business school graduates. She was sick of it. How could it be just business if it affected people's lives? It was always personal. Like this moment.

Clementine decided she would clean her face—but only because The Owl was nice enough to tell her about it. She liked the Director of Human Resources. Clementine hoped The Owl had a nest full of baby owls in her apartment, so she could teach them all to be just as decent. The world needed more thoughtful birds of a feather.

There was a bottle of water in her purse. Half drunk. It was left over from the last conference meeting she led, which she thought she kicked ass in. She pulled some tissues from the box she was leaving for the new occupant, who would take over her much coveted office tomorrow, and poured a little bit of water on them. As she wiped the blackness off her, she thought of all the possible misread signs and miscalculated moves she made in her short career as the Creative Director of the biggest advertising agency in the world.

She had navigated the path of her corporate career with as much confidence as a two-hundred-dollar session with her psychic, Cassandra, could buy. Last year, during one of her beneficial months, Cassandra advised her to ask for a raise. She did and got it. When lucky Jupiter was in her sign (or whatever Cassandra called it), she was told her presentation to a new client would yield a lucrative deal. It did. So how did she end up here? Was her psychic losing her special power?

Clementine always thought of psychic power as a natural, born-into ability a few were given—like being Superman or Wonder Woman. But maybe it was more of a finite phenomenon, like a spring that could one day dry up. She looked at The Owl and wondered if she had any special powers. The woman was as patient as a boulder while she watched Clementine slowly removing the signs of weakness and shame from her face. She must have been trained in the special task of handling broken spirits and guiding them toward the light…of the outside.

"Has IT come by to collect everything?" The Owl asked.

"Yes. They took my phone, laptop, and badge."

She reminded herself those items were not hers anymore. They never were. She was just passing through. She was no more than a seasonal laborer like an apple picker or a sweater stacker at Macy's during the holidays. Her life here—the long hours, the stress, the politics that kept her up nights—was reduced to one box. In it was a stress ball with the blue bunny logo (also her idea), a book she was reading while she ate lunch, three prestigious awards for the advertising campaigns she led, a pair of ballet flats, her tote, and a label maker she bought with her own money. The Owl eyed the label maker, wondering whether it was the company's property, but was too nice to ask.

"I brought it from home," Clementine said.

"Oh, I wasn't—"

"It's okay. I would have wondered the same thing."

She picked up the box and straightened her back as if a string was pulling her head up to the sky. Her mom used to say that she was always living in the clouds.

"Please follow me," The Owl said.

Clementine willed herself to not take one last look at her office. It was not hers anymore. It never was.

As she walked through the building decorated in knock-off mid-century-modern furniture, she felt stares on her like jagged knives. She did not meet them. She was sure some were kind, but those were almost worse. Instead she kept her eyes fixed on the back of the matching pink sweater set belonging to the HR Director. She tried to imagine how it would feel to lead someone to a certain death like the masked headsman of yore. She thought it ironic how the executioner who did the beheading was called a headsman when his job was to take heads away. Maybe it was because he had so many.

They continued walking in the funeral procession of two until they reached the HR department. The Owl opened the door to her office and pointed to a seat. Clementine saw the name Amelia on the door. Not at all owlish.

She sat down and kept the box on her lap, guarding it with the possessiveness of a cat with its fresh kill. The HR director walked to the other side of the desk and took her seat. She opened a folder with Clementine's name on it and pulled out a thick packet. She turned it around and slid it in front of her.

"What is it?"

"The details of your severance package. Directors get one."

"You mean I'm not the only one?"

"I'm not at liberty to discuss other employees with you. It's just a move toward consolidation. To flatten the reporting structure. It's business. Not a personal attack against you or your work."

That eight-letter-word again. *Business. Business. Business.* It sounded like fingernails on chalkboard.

"You mean to increase the bottom line?" Clementine did not even try to hide the contempt in her voice.

Amelia answered with a gentle smile.

"If you could please read it and sign your acknowledgement and acceptance."

"Right now?"

"You may take it home or have your lawyer look at it. But your severance package won't be dispensed until it's signed. You have two weeks to review and make a decision to accept or decline."

"What are the terms of my severance?"

"Among other things, a year's pay. It's pretty generous, if you ask me."

Amelia leaned forward and looked at Clementine with her big wise eyes. "You can consider it a gift or a misfortune. It's up to you."

Outside, the sky was in shades of pinks and oranges. Clementine navigated the tourist filled sidewalk with the self-possession of a seasoned New Yorker until she realized the backs of her feet were blistering. She had forgotten to exchange her pointy heels for the ballet flats. She hobbled to a planter and teetered the box on one knee while performing the circus maneuver of shoe swapping.

"Clementine?" a familiar voice above asked.

She closed her eyes. She guessed the prayer she made to the patron saint of please-don't-let-me-see-someone-I-know was ignored. She opened them.

"Fuck," she said. It was her ex-boyfriend Mike. Mark. Whatever his name was.

When the shit rained, the shit poured. Clementine was soaked in it.

"Nice to see you too," said ex-boyfriend-Mark. "What are you doing in this part of the city?"

"I'm meeting someone." In her haste she had forgotten to take the long way around the block to avoid him. He got this territory as per Article One of their break-up agreement.

Mark peered into the box and smiled that same smile she used to like but now had the urge to punch off his face.

"Interesting things to bring to a meeting. Lots of awards. Were some of these the result of neglecting your relationships?"

"Fuck off, Mark. I'm busy." She forced her swollen feet into her shoes and continued walking. Her blisters were keeping her from running.

Mark followed. "Oh, come on. I was just kidding. It's been a long time. Don't you want to talk to your old friend?"

"A friend would not have burned the clothes I left in his apartment and had them messengered to my office."

"What can I say, I'm a passionate man. I thought that's what you liked about me."

She looked at him with narrowed eyes. "Some of those were expensive."

He waved his hand in the air like he was shooing away a fly. "Bygones."

"Why are you still following me?" she asked.

"Where are you going?"

"None of your business."

"Wait, you're not going to—oh you are!" he said.

"Shut up."

"You're still wasting money on that old cooch?"

"Classy. As per usual."

"Did she foresee this too? She should have told you to bring a rolling luggage to work."

"You're an asshole."

Mark laughed. Clementine really wanted to knock out his teeth. If only her hands were not full. She was glad she had dumped him. She could not remember why she had gone out with him in the first place.

"What if you let me help you carry the box until you get to

Cassandra's place?"

"No, thank you."

"You can't still be mad about the clothes."

Clementine stopped. "Fuck the clothes. It was a bad break up on top of a bad year and I'd rather not relive it on one of the worst days of my life. So, if you could just go back home or to wherever you were headed, I'd appreciate it."

Pain crossed Mark's face. Without another word he turned and walked the other way.

"Typical," she said under her breath and continued her walk.

It really was not all his fault she hated him. He was not a bad boyfriend. He could be thoughtful, funny, even charming. But when they were together, she found herself constantly annoyed by him. His hovering. His voice. His persistent "Are you okay?" He was unbearable. Being irritated by him became a habit she could not shake. Months later and the rage she felt in his presence was still as irrational and palpable. It was as if she had focused everything negative that happened that year into one spot—and that spot was on his face.

Cassandra's home, which she also used to receive clients, was on the third story of an old brownstone. A psychologist's office was on the second floor and a lawyer's office was on the first. It was a one stop shop for the broken hearted. Clementine thought of the thick paperwork in her tote. Maybe she could get the lawyer to look at it.

The door was open.

"Lucy, I'm home!" Clementine yelled upon seeing the shocking curly rust-colored hair peeking above the box in her hands.

"For god's sake, pipe down! The psychiatrist is having her weekly session," the psychic whispered loudly as she ushered Clementine in.

"What is it this week? Apeirophobia, Achluophobia, Ailurophobia?"

Cassandra rolled her eyes and closed the door of her apartment.

"Leave that box in the foyer, I don't want its bad juju in my psychic space."

She looked Clementine up and down. "You're gonna need a cleansing. Your aura is all icky."

"My soul is icky."

"Your soul is not icky. This is temporary."

"I thought you were going to tell me 'this too shall pass,'" Clementine said.

"That's a nice saying."

"It doesn't suit you."

Cassandra scoffed. "I see you're still as peppery as ever. What happened to the cry baby from earlier?"

"She was murdered in the office of an HR director in a pink sweater set."

The psychic raised an eyebrow. "That bad?"

"No, it wasn't that bad. I thought it would hurt more—being blindsided and all."

She narrowed her eyes at her psychic. At two-hundred-dollars a session she was not supposed to be blindsided by anything.

"I know you blame me for not seeing this coming. I did see a major change, but I guess I didn't apply it to your job, seeing how hard you work. Hardworking people aren't supposed to lose their jobs," said Cassandra.

"Maybe in your time," Clementine said and shrugged. "But by the end it felt a little bit like closure. The woman has a gift with people. Well, at least me. They should pay her a lot more money and never let her go."

Cassandra led her into the room next to the foyer. It was a cozy space with a large window that overlooked a tree lined street. In the day time it was bright and airy. But at night the psychic kept the curtains closed to hide the space from evil spirits. A tiered chandelier made of mother-of-pearl disks lit the space like the inside of a jewelry box.

Clementine plopped onto a comfortable cream-colored couch. Cassandra took a spot on the lime mohair chair opposite. On the mahogany table next to them were two tea cups hand painted with roses and ivy. In them was coffee, still piping hot. The psychic thought tea was for sissies and old ladies. She was old, but no lady.

Clementine loved this space. It felt safe, like a warm hug. She shrugged off her shoes and stretched out on the sofa. The chandelier above looked like a hundred full moons.

A long sigh escaped her. She began to feel the coil inside unwinding. With no bandages holding it together, the fissure in her heart was leaking blood again. It had nothing to do with the job nor the lack of it, she knew.

Above her, she saw a hand holding a bundle of dried up sage with white smoke unfurling from one end. The hand slowly waved it over her body from the top of her head to the tip of her toes, making her feel like roast meat. The scent of burning sage permeated the air.

Cassandra mumbled something unintelligible. Probably a Wiccan chant. Clementine felt her foot twitching from impatience. She was not here for the energy cleansing, but she could not stop the ceremony. It would have been rude. Next, Cassandra pinched the air with her hand and proceeded to pluck the ickiness from Clementine's aura like a mother hen pecking at worms. It went on for ten minutes. Her aura needed deep cleansing.

When the psychic was done, Clementine sat up. She did not want to waste any more time being scrubbed. Her aura felt raw.

"Can I talk to my mom?" she asked.

She needed her mom on one of the worst days of her life. Her mother had died more than a year ago, around the same time the window fell from the 27th floor. One had nothing to do with the other. They only shared the same space in time.

"We can try," Cassandra said and lit a candle on the coffee table.

There was never a guarantee when it came to spirits. They were fickle and busy creatures, given to whims that could change at a moment's notice. Wouldn't you be if you could travel at the speed of thought to any realm and planet?

The psychic chanted a long incantation in Latin that Clementine did not understand. Clementine wondered whether Latin was a requisite for all spirits and ghosts. Was there a crash course everyone had to take once dead?

When it ended, Cassandra began speaking in English. "May the spirit of Marjorie come forth to her daughter, Clementine."

The candle flickered.

"She's here."

"Mom?"

"She says you look tired. She's wondering if you've been sleeping. The weather is turning and she wants you to wear warmer clothes."

Clementine smiled. It was typical of her mother to fuss over her as if she was a child. She could hear her mother's voice in her ears. *Dress warmer! Eat your vegetables! Do your homework! Stop chewing your nails!*

"It's been a rough week. Lost my job today."

"She's cursing." After a long pause Cassandra continued, "She says those assholes—excuse my French—don't know what they lost. You can give her the names of the people you want haunted. She knows some ghosts that owe her favors."

"No, mom. No need to put a hit on them. I'll be fine."

"She wishes she could give you a hug. Oh, she asked me to hug you for her."

The psychic and Clementine leaned toward each other and embraced. Cassandra's body was hot and the fragrance on her skin striking. It was sweet and floral like a walk through Saks' perfume department. Clementine felt a wetness on the psychic's shoulder and realized it was from her own tears. When she pulled back she saw Cassandra's warm smile.

"Don't worry, I never wear fabric that can't get wet when I see you," the psychic said and touched her cheek.

Clementine smiled shyly and wiped her eyes. "What's it like on the other side?"

Cassandra tilted her head to one side, listening.

"The light is brighter and the dark is darker. All the colors are more vivid. It's like living inside perfectly edited Instagram photos. All the time."

"Must be overwhelming."

"You have no idea, baby girl."

Clementine liked it when her mother called her that. It evoked memories of all that was good and nice in the world: summertime, falling snowflakes, the scent of fresh waffle cones, and strangely, baby powder.

"So, what did you do all day?"

"She said her day is not made up of twenty-four hours like ours. Time actually doesn't matter at all. And she doesn't sleep so it's hard for her to quantify a day."

Clementine rolled her eyes. "You don't have to be so literal."

"Well, she said before she came here she was in Central Park. But it was not the Central Park of today. It was winter then. Sometime during the turn of the century. The one before last. The women were skating in their long dresses and fur coats and the men wore suits and bowler hats. Everything was covered in snow. The park looked like a winter wonderland. She knows she was not supposed to feel the cold being dead, but she did anyway. It's funny what the mind remembers."

Clementine closed her eyes and saw the image behind her lids. It was black, white, and gray—an antique photograph. Her mother used to bring her to skate at Wollman Rink in the fall and winter. At night they glided on the ice, surrounded by the twinkling lights of the city and the starry sky. She had not gone back since her mother died.

"And before that?" she asked.

"She was on one of the moons of Jupiter. She wasn't sure which one. Callisto. Elara. Europa. Lysithea. Io…"

"Okay, now you're just showing off," said Clementine. "What was it like?"

"Cloudy."

Clementine laughed. Then she wondered who her mother went to all these places with. She was never good at being alone.

"Are you dating anyone?"

"Hmm. She's not saying anything."

"Why not?"

"She said a lady is always discreet."

Clementine paused. She felt tears coming.

"Tell me everything will be okay," she asked in a small voice.

"Everything will be okay. She's proud of who you are—the woman you've become. Smart. Driven. Responsible. She's confident you'll have it all figured out in no time. If not, you have a year to do whatever you want."

"How do you—"

"She said she snuck a look at the paperwork when you weren't paying attention. Your mom is sneaky."

"Yeah, she's always been."

Clementine opened her eyes and let out a loud exhale, emptying her lungs. She knew it in her heart, just as her mom and Cassandra said, that she would be fine. Her legs were just as strong as they were yesterday, her mind just as capable, her hands just as able. Everything about her was powerful enough to hold the weight of life, just as it always was. The world felt good again.

# Dust Bound

Bangkok, Thailand, 2017

*The golden dunes lay silent—a sleeping woman. The curves of her body ripple like waves across the waterless ocean. A desert so vast an outsider could spend his entire life getting lost in—as dangerous and enticing as a lover's embrace. The nomadic people of the land, the Bedouin, call this place home.*

"You want more coffee?" a uniformed young woman asked in heavily accented English, startling Ali out of concentration.

"What? No, no thanks," he answered in the distracted way of an absentminded professor.

Blood drained out of her face. Ali realized he must have sounded as if he was irritated. He knew he sometimes talked in the clipped, rapid way of an impatient New Yorker. It was a hard habit to shake.

He made his best effort at a smile. The waitress's pale face turned the color of rose apple as if someone had dropped red food coloring into cake batter. He wondered what he did wrong. His hand went to his beard. Maybe his mother was right that it was time for a shave.

The girl turned about-face and walked off. The other waitresses, women just as young in the same yellow and black uniforms, swarmed her. Muted chatter in Thai rose from the group. Ali's eyebrows scrunched together. For one moment he was confused. He looked around and realized he was in a coffee shop in Bangkok, not Café Grumpy on Twentieth and Eighth.

Then why was the girl speaking English to him? That was what threw him off. He scanned the crowd once more to be sure. Black heads of hair dominated the place, peppered by a few light ones. Outside, on the other side of the large windows, was a dusty scene of cars, trucks, and motorcycles in a monstrous gridlock. The glaring sun above shone bright, making the floating specks look like sparkling diamond particles. The image was like a hazy sun-bleached photograph—beautiful from the shelter of this café. Yes, he was in Thailand.

He had been back in the country of his birth for a few months now, yet he still felt displaced. He thought it ironic that he would feel foreign in his motherland. But it was not as if he could help it. He went to NYU for longer than deemed respectable for a Bachelor of Arts. Before that, he was at a fancy boarding school upstate. He had lived in New York longer than he had lived anywhere else. It had left a rind on him.

He shifted his attention back to the book.

*Water is their obsession. The search for it begins before one is born and ends after one is dead. Life revolves around it. Every Bedouin learns from a young age the exact locations of the wells and springs between destinations. They know almost by instinct to watch the flight of birds and listen to their twittering for clues of water. In the heat of the summer, they migrate toward oases and rain clouds. The last comes with danger, but it matters not, for there is nothing worse than death from thirst.*

He picked up his cup of coffee and drained it. A drop escaped his lips and disappeared into his beard. He thought maybe it really was his facial hair that led the waitresses to think he was a foreigner. After all, it did mask half his face. When his mother first saw him at the airport, she commented that he looked like a northern Indian. There was some Middle Eastern blood in his family tree somewhere generations back that lingered in his features. The wavy hair, the olive skin, the big eyes, the long nose. They did not do him a favor living in America after 9/11. For a long time he kept his face well-shaven. He only began growing a beard when it came into style with the hipsters and after half the men in Chelsea had one.

The Bedouin men in the old black and white photographs he had seen had facial hair. Ali imagined a beard would come in handy during a sandstorm as an added shield against pelting sand. Bangkok did not have sandstorms but it did have a horrendous smog problem, with a permanent brown layer covering everything like a thin film of tar.

He noticed something on the right bottom margin of the page—a flowy Thai script written faintly in pencil as if the person did not want to mar the book more than necessary.

*'Is the heat of the desert as suffocating as that of a monsoon summer? Would one hold closer the fear of God and monsters when thirst is constant?'*

Ali wondered who wrote it. The book came from the house he now owned. He found it amongst the dusty tomes on the shelves in a library underneath the eaves. The house had been in his family since the late forties but was left empty after his parents moved before he was born. His father and mother made a fortune in land and now lived in a modern mansion on a posh street near the embassies of the world.

Their house was only a twenty-minute walk from his, yet it was a world away. It had central air conditioning and three maids. The three maids—'aunties' as he called them—were the reason he decided to move out of his parents' house and into his own. They had been with his mother for so long, they were practically family. The women, all unmarried, were always buzzing about, moving his things, and reprimanding him as if he was a child. It was as though he had four mothers. For someone used to having privacy and total control of his daily life, having four mothers was more than he could handle.

The old house was in Kampong Java, an Indonesian enclave in the heart of Bangkok. His parents had given it to him as an early wedding present. Premature, to be precise. He did not even have a prospect yet. But that did not stop his mother from vocalizing her wish for that to soon change.

Ali loved the house. At least from the outside. It was a two-story with wood siding painted the color of milky turquoise. Dressing the edges of the eaves was white gingerbread filigree—a nod to European colonial architecture even though Thailand was never colonized. In the garden, a banyan tree, with fine harp-like strings shooting down from its branches and large intertwining roots the size of Burmese pythons, took up most of the front yard. It fanned its big, bright green leaves like a gigantic multi-tiered umbrella over the grounds. Big-leaf ferns, pygmy palms, and other plants which he could not name, peppered the garden.

The inside was a different story. It was a hollow space with multiple rooms interconnecting like a maze. The curtains, older than him, were moth-eaten and smelled of mildew. The few pieces of furniture in the house were constructed of heavy, ornate woods—left there because they were too bulky to move. The emptiness of the space unsettled him, yet he related to it in ways he could not explain. His relationship with the house, like others in his life, was complicated.

A different girl in uniform came to stand next to his table.

"Excuse me, sir," she said in English. She sounded more confident than the last girl. At least she tried to.

Like the other waitress, she thought he was foreign. He decided not to correct her. They embarrassed easily at this age.

"Yes?" Ali said, trying so hard to be extra friendly that his cheeks hurt.

"You want food?" She slid a laminated menu in front of him with a smile.

He looked at his watch. 1 o'clock. He had been here longer than he thought. That was probably the reason the waitresses were anxious to feed him. They were like the three aunties. He could hear them now. *Are you hungry? Let me make you food. You're too skinny.* And his own mother in the background—*when are you going to make me a grandma?*

He looked at the menu. Each item was a large image with its name in big English writing underneath. Soon they would be reverting to communicating with hieroglyphs. Were emojis not already the *lingua franca* of today?

He pointed to the picture of shrimp omelet over rice. It was a mild simple dish he thought an unadventurous non-Thai might order. Why not, he could try this persona on for size. He could be anyone he wanted for the day. Nobody knew him.

The girl thanked him, took the menu and walked off. The other employees surrounded her like a school of yellow and black fish, swallowing her back into the Andaman Sea. Another hushed chatter followed. When they noticed him looking their way, they all covered their mouths and giggled. He could not help but smile. Their innocence was sweet. It was not how teenage girls acted where he came from.

Where he came from… He realized then he thought New York was home. How could one see home as a place where one's residency was dependent on a student visa? He wondered what time it was in New York. He sighed and went back to the book.

*To the Bedouin, the desert is not mysterious. It is known, even in the dark. The intense heat of the sun forces them to travel mostly at night, navigating with stars and the shapes of mountains. They do not need maps. They know the barren hills like the bodies of their wives.*

*Besides water, their nomadic life revolves around the search for grazing land for their animals. They migrate with the seasons, carrying portable goatskin tents to the fringes of the desert where their flocks can forage on dew-fed pastures. After the rain in the spring, they venture into the heart of the desert to feed their animals on new shoots. But the main migrations are between the summer pasture near the mountains in the north and the winter pasture in the south.*

"Your food," a voice spoke. Ali looked up and saw a different waitress. In her hand was a plate of shrimp omelet over rice.

"Can you please bring me a bottle of water and another coffee?" he asked. Reading about the Bedouin made him thirsty.

A confused look crossed her face.

He repeated slowly. "Water and coffee?"

Her eyes grew wider from understanding. "Oh. Yes."

"Thank you."

He was beginning to think it was a bad idea to let the waitresses think he could not speak Thai. Now he would never be able to speak Thai here. If they ever find out, they would think he was mocking them, or that he was pretentious. But he was in too deep. At this point, he just had to let it play out. He wondered how a simple act of forgetting where he was had led him to this web of lies.

The crispy, garlicky scent of the omelet made him salivate. He took a bite. The texture was fluffy, unlike the dense American version, which he never liked. The shrimp, diced and mixed in with the garlic, had a nice crust on it. He ate another spoonful and continued reading.

*The desert dwellers pray to God, the same God who grants life and water. They stand toward the Kaaba and prostrate in a mosque with a carpet of sand and a ceiling of sky. They perform ablution with dry dust and sacrifice animals for food with the name of Allah at their lips.*

At the word 'sacrifice,' Ali remembered he had once witnessed a *Qurban*, the ritual animal sacrifice at the mosque. When he was little—he could not remember at what age—he insisted that his father bring him to see it. The cow was reddish brown with large eyes on the sides of its head. One man stood in the front, petting its neck, soothing it. The other stood next to its flank, holding its middle. Another man held the rope tight in his hand. In a loose circle around it was a throng of faces watching with various expressions. He remembered thinking the cow was brave. He would not have been as calm under the crowd's intense stares.

The act was quick. The large sharp knife came and went like the snap of a finger. In the name of God and it was done. The cow collapsed onto the floor, and afterward, the only evidence left was a thin spray of blood on his shirt, a bowl of beef curry his dad took home to his mom, and a trail of tears on his face.

He had never watched an animal being killed since. In America, he purchased his meat packaged and perfect inside the glaring white luminescence of the supermarket. He even bought it chopped so he did not have to run a knife through it. There was a separation between the meat and him until he ate it. Sterile. Godless.

A cup of coffee and a bottle of water were placed in front of him. He looked up and saw a different waitress than the last. He smiled, thanked her and read on.

*Out in the openness, their fear is magnified. There are monsters. The monsters of the desert. The Jinns and the Ahl Al-ard prey on lone travelers. They turn souls black and suck out the heart's blood.*

*The Bedouin pay heed to the stories told to them in the same way their grandparents had. They travel in large groups. They tear strips of prayer clothes to mark trees and entrances to caves where spirits live. The life of a nomad is free, but there's a price for freedom.*

Ali was no stranger to stories of Jinns. While the children in the West were told fairytales, he was told stories about monsters and ghosts. Created by God from smokeless fire, they can assume any form they desire. Some were demonic and would haunt graveyards at night to prey on human flesh. Others would whisper into ears and cause a man's heart to go astray. He used to be so afraid of the Jinns. He was not entirely sure he was completely free of the fear.

He saw the same handwriting in the margin.

*'A change of names, and God and monsters are just as terrifying whether in the middle of the desert or a city.'*

Ali did not agree. He had never been paralyzed by the fear of God, but he had been of monsters. A few times in his life he had experienced something the Thais called ghost possession—not quite the kind that required an exorcism, although no less terrifying. It always happened in bed in the early morning hours when the top of the sun first touched the horizon. He would feel a presence on him, sitting on his chest. Sometimes the presence was next to him on the bed. But he never saw it. It was the thing that lived just beyond the corners of his eyes. Then he would feel something that he could only best describe as a slow intrusion into his body, like water seeping into clay. When it happened, he could not move. His body was strung into the bed as if someone had sewn tiny threads around it. Try as he might to scream, he could not. There were times he was confident the sound he pushed out from his throat had escaped, but it never did. He was helpless.

Ali was not a religious man, but in those moments, he called on God. He would read one of the few *surahs* he could remember from the Qur'an—the one about Jinns his mother said would protect him from evil spirits. Eventually, after a few rounds of the verses, the feeling would disappear, and he would regain the control of his body again. When he got older, he learned the phenomenon was called sleep paralysis.

He wondered if the owner of the faint handwriting was a family member. From the loose flowy style, he assumed it belonged to a woman. She once lived at the house, he was certain. No one would write on a book owned by someone else. To put down a name, a thought or a drawing into a book was the utmost personal act one could do to it.

He felt like naming the mysterious woman, giving her an identity, like she had with her thoughts in the book. Something classic. As he chewed, he pondered the list of women in his life. Nothing seemed fitting. Before he knew it, the plate was clean.

A waitress, a new one, materialized next to him as if she had been waiting for her cue on a stage play. He looked around, wondering how many waitresses they had at this café. They just kept coming out like they were produced by a factory machine in the back. Discomfort increased at the thought of the number of women he was now deceiving. Five so far by his count. Although who knew how many more poor, sweet waitresses were privy to the information.

"You finished?" she asked with an eager smile.

Guilt rose at the thought of not speaking Thai. He decided he would say as little as he could, so he only nodded. As the girl cleared his table, he looked at her name tag for inspiration. *Bussaba.* A classic Thai name meaning flower.

He tried it on for size, imagining a twenty-something woman, a bookworm, sitting in the loft under the eaves of the house, burrowing into her favorite reading spot where the sun made a square shape through the window. In her hand was a book—this book. She flipped the pages and it made a crisp sound, the kind of sound a new book makes. She did not seem like a Bussaba, but he liked the thought of a flower.

There was a name he had always liked that was neither Thai, Indonesian, nor Arabic. Lily. Could the mystery woman be a Lily?

"You want coffee?" the waitress asked, his dirty plate and cup in her hand.

He nodded. Everything out of his mouth would support the lie that was continuing to grow the longer he sat here. Its heaviness was slowly sinking into his stomach. Maybe he should leave, he thought. But there was still the cup of coffee he had just ordered. He really did not need another cup of coffee. He only nodded from guilt. It was a tic, really.

He felt as though he was always in a perpetual cycle of feeling guilty because he had deceived someone. Often it started out as something minuscule and accidental, even well-intentioned, like this quandary he was in. Then, like a rain stain, it would grow into something increasingly difficult to ignore until it sprouted mold and choked the air with toxic spores. Once in college, he told a girl she was pretty. He said it because he thought she looked sad. One thing led to another and they ended up going out for months. All that time he was not remotely attracted to her. Eventually, she broke up with him. Her reason was simple. She told him she did it because he had been too much of a coward to do it himself. He was grateful.

Perhaps guilt and deception were a permanent part of him, like a genetic defect. Maybe he was a closeted liar. Or maybe it was not hidden at all and everyone could see through him and knew he was a chronic deceiver. Only they were too polite to say.

If he really thought about it, the three aunties were not the real reason he moved out of his parents' house. With so many pairs of eyes on him, he felt as if he was made of cellophane. Everyone—his father, his mother, his little sister, the three aunties, and now the five waitresses—could see right through him into his heart and soul. What did they see? Did they hate what they saw?

But what was he really? He had spent so much time living his life in-between places, in that gap things fell into and got lost, that he was not even sure who he was. The only thing he was sure of was his name—a given name he had learned to inhabit. He wondered if the woman he called Lily would like the name he had given her.

He flipped through the book, looking for more notes, as if in them he could find clues to answer whether she would like her name. He had almost missed it. In the margin on page 111, he saw her handwriting. It was faint like all the others. But instead of the usual complete thought, it was a single word posed as a question. He looked at the section of the book it pertained to.

*Somewhere buried under the wasteland of the empty quarter is the city of Iram, entered only by the uninitiated through the secret door of dreams. It was created by a tribe of giants and hidden by God. Although some said Iram is not a physical place but a parallel reality. There, one could commune with the Jinns and the Old Ones of the desert. Through Iram, one could walk the path toward Annihilation, a state of absolute destruction, where one is absorbed into the Void and becomes one with God.*

Ali imagined a desolate desert where the sky was covered with coal-colored clouds that held no rain. A vast expanse of shape-shifting sand dunes and jagged boulders where there were no oases, not even a single tree. A dark and foreboding place where monsters roamed. So why did Lily choose the word to associate with this place, even if it was a question?

The one-word question fascinated him. Not for the word itself but for the possible reasons it was chosen. He reread the paragraph, dissecting it, trying to make the connection. Was it the last word—God—that led her to think such a thought? Or maybe it was the fear. Could the appeal of Iram be the fear of the mystical unknown attached to it? Humans were designed to fear. Or maybe it was the complete destruction of self that attracted her. What could be purer or more honest than nothingness?

Ali stared at the one-word question. The word grew and contracted as if his eyes were camera lenses trying to focus. His mind revisited everything he had read thus far in the book. He tried to understand the enigmatic woman within the context of her life—Kampong Java, the old Thailand, her faith. Then it dawned on him the real reason he moved into the old house. It was the same reason he was both afraid of and drawn to it. It was not the annoyance of the three aunties, the lack of privacy, nor the x-ray eyes of those surrounding him. It was the allure of starting anew in the familiarity of the old. The Kampong Java house was big and empty, but filled with his family's memories, like the great desert of mystery and history that attracted the Bedouin for millennia. It was Ali's city of Iram.

He felt a presence next to him. Another waitress. Another a cup of coffee.

"*Khob khun krub*," he thanked her. For one moment he froze. He did not even plan to say it. The words rolled off him as if they were always at the tip of his tongue, waiting for their turn to make an appearance.

The girl's eyes were wide with wonder. "Your Thai very good."

He smiled and looked at Lily's single word question. Through it was a gate and through that gate were possibilities.

# The Woman in the Garden

San Diego, U.S.A., 2011

A camera doesn't lie. It captures a slice of life as is. The way a lens redirects light as it travels through layers of atmosphere and bounces off an object to form an image is a physical, definite thing. From behind a lens, a photographer sees the truth. Before perception. Before the editing process. Before enhancements. From this place, the world is raw and honest, shouting, 'SEE ME!' But not everyone does. Or wants to. Why is that?

In my hand is a photograph of a woman nobody believes exists. In the photo, she is standing in a neglected garden surrounded by brown-yellow grass that grazes her knees. The background, an expansive ocean, is the color of azure glass. The sun sits low behind her, haloing her unruly mane and outlining her body garbed in a shapeless pale frock of thin fabric.

Her white hair, fine as silk and thick as a down blanket, reaches her waist. The few loose strands flying around her face tell me the image was taken just as the wind was blowing. My memory tells me the cool wind—much appreciated on a stifling day when the air was dry like the inside of a Tandoori oven—blew from the direction of the Pacific.

On her face, an indecipherable smile. In her hand, a flower. The light touches it in a way that obscures its exact hue. I know, however, that the house, where I had taken this picture, has a porch with climbing roses the color of cream with a touch of strawberry juice. So, I could assume from that bit of logic that the flower is a rose and the rose is of that shade.

The picture does not show this, but the house was built a long time ago. It is an arts-and-crafts cottage from the beginning of the nineteen-hundreds, with a history and a language different from those that surround it. Perched on a cliff at the tip of La Jolla, a sleepy enclave of the affluent, it is an unassuming house compared to its neighbors. The specs state it has two bedrooms and one bathroom with a footprint of eight hundred square feet. It nestles between a sprawling faux-Tuscan mansion owned by an infamous corporate lawyer serving time for a white-collar crime, and a ghastly Bauhaus atrocity belonging to a wealthy billionaire perpetually stuck in the air.

I know the house, though only in the superficial, fleeting way a photographer knows a model. For example, I know the living room has wood paneling and two built-in bookcases on either side of the stone fireplace. Its bathroom has an antique toilet with a wall-mounted tank and a pull chain flush, the kind in old European bed and breakfasts. The small kitchen, with its Shaker style wood cabinets and gray stone countertops, is more handsome from its lack of a dishwasher. The master bedroom has a desk that looks out to the overgrown garden and the sea. This is my favorite spot, as I imagine it's hers.

I don't know why but I feel like I know the woman. She is as tangible to me as the strong scent of lemon oil and disinfectant in the cottage. There is something eerily familiar about her—the white hair, the earnest brown eyes, even her Mona Lisa-like smile. It's as if we are somehow connected, tethered to each other like two ends of a tin can telephone. But what's the message? Why to only me?

I wished to ask her but she had vanished. Like a blown-out candle. Like an apparition.

You may wonder whether I am mad—like the Mad Hatter from Alice in Wonderland. Or if I'm a liar. The people I showed the photo to thought so. They—the partners of the real estate firm who hired me for the project, the 'Tweedles'—laughed as if what I saw, what I had documented, is an impossibility. It is as if the proof in my hand does not matter.

They told me no one lives in the house. It has stood vacant since the owner moved away to Connecticut, leaving it unoccupied for the last year.

Does the owner have a mother who comes by occasionally to tend to the garden? I had asked. No, the owner has no family here, they had answered. What about neighbors, anyone who would care enough to pull weeds and tend the flower bed? No, nobody cares about a miniscule house hidden behind two mansions. The owner, underwater and upside down after the diseased subprime mortgage exploded in puss, wants it sold as soon as possible. Your job is to take pictures, not ask questions.

I had demanded that they look closely at the photo. It was taken in the backyard of the house. The woman exists, or existed, at least in that specific moment she was captured by my camera. The truth is there, in physical form, staring into their eyes like the woman was staring into mine.

They said a photo can be manipulated. A lie can be told with tools of deception. The old hag is no one, they said in a tone that indicated it was *me* who was no one. As I looked into their faces painted with sneers, I remember wondering what it would feel like to be in their privileged position. To own the mocking blue eyes. To expel the suppressed laughter. To always have my words be heard. To be seen.

There is a pain you get when someone calls your truth a lie—right below your heart, where the xiphoid process meets the diaphragm. A pinching, sharp pang of a nail driven into bone. It takes your breath away. I thought I'd be used to it by now, this sensation, but there is always a new facet to be discovered. When you keep your wounds green, they never heal.

So, here I am again—this being the only place answers can be unearthed. The driveway is hidden away from the street behind tall trees. I parked my car two blocks away so not to draw questions from any passing neighbors. Not that there are many. The rich have homes like normal people have purses, so the neighborhood is quiet but for the tweeting of birds in their nests. It is private—a perfect sanctuary.

I unlock the front door with the key from the lockbox and place it back. In the serene, shadow-filled cottage, the late afternoon light filters through the slats between the plantation shutters, stretching out slender fingers on the wood floor. In soft steps, I make my way to the desk in the master bedroom. I don't even know what I should be looking for. Another photograph, perhaps? Maybe a journal? Something.

I place the photo on the desk and look out the window. The overgrown garden is no more. There is now a bright yellow excavator next to a large hole in the ground. The image makes me sad. The Tweedles said the owner wants to add a swimming pool to increase its salability. At twenty to thirty thousand to add an inground pool, he must be desperate to sell.

I open the first drawer of the desk. The only content inside is a set of keys. They are painted with different color dots on each, probably nail polish. The colors are pretty and not at all generic—crimson, eggplant, fuchsia, even midnight blue. The second drawer contains instruction manuals and warrantees for random electronics. The third has a book on San Diego gardening. After a year of vacancy, I should not have expected there to be much left in terms of personal effects.

I switch my attention to the rest of the room, searching under the bed and in the drawers of the side tables, finding only dust bunnies and cobwebs. Sweat drips down my temples and I wipe it hastily, ignoring my own plea to open a window and let in the cool ocean air. I cannot leave any trail.

The glare of the setting sun slips through the leaves of a tree and pierces my eyes, blurring my vision with a burst of orange light. I turn my head, pained by its unsympathetic journey toward the horizon. I'm running out of time.

I go back to the desk and take the keys from the first drawer. There are many locks in any house. And this house, with its built-ins and odd-shaped rooms, has many for its size. There has to be something here that can reveal the mystery of the woman.

I move through the cottage, room by room, searching drawers and cabinets, only to find nothing more than meaningless paperwork and inkless pens. In the living room, empty bookshelves stand lonely like hollowed sacks with no souls. For a moment I feel sad for the cottage and the old woman. The owner, like a hermit crab who had outgrown its shell, had escaped with everything that meant something to him. My eyes flit to the object above the mantle I had not seen before.

*All except for an oil painting.*

The image warms against the white plaster wall. It is a generic landscape of the Central California desert with rolling hills of mustard yellow and globe-shaped olive-green oak trees. On the bottom right hand corner is a signature, a name.

*Is it her?*

"Margaret Duras," I say the name as I stare at the painting in the spot where the shadow meets the trees.

An electric current travels spine to crown, making the hair on the back of my neck stand at attention. I feel a weight on my left shoulder, anchoring me in place. I move my hand to the spot the weight rests, and find the softness of a palm. It is as warm as the heat of the dying sun, and pale against my sienna skin. I slowly turn my head and look behind me. The face of the woman with the Mona Lisa smile greets. I smile back to let her know that I know she is real, that she has always been real to me since the moment I saw her. Tears begin to cloud my eyes as I let the truth of Margaret's existence wash through, imbuing me with its strength.

Without a word she takes my hand and pulls me away from the painting and the living room. She waits as I open the door to the backyard before leading me out. As she passes the unsightly hole in the ground, she stares at it accusingly as if offended by its presence.

We turn the corner to the side of the house and stop in front of a

117

door hidden behind a flowering camellia bush that I had not seen in my previous visit. The door sits at a forty-five-degree angle—half against the house, half against the ground like a tornado shelter that belongs in a Midwestern home. She looks at me and I know what she wants. I search through the keys in my hand and pick the one with the midnight blue dot. I unlock the door and pull it open.

There are steps leading down to a dark basement. The only natural light source, a small window on the opposite wall. I feel for a light switch. When I turn it on, the blue-tinged fluorescent light above brightens the room. Margaret takes my hand and ushers me down the stairs. Once my feet find the landing, the door bangs closed behind me and I jump, almost hitting my head against the low ceiling.

The basement is about the size of the above living room and the dining room combined. It is neat and well-organized with boxes labeled with numbers and descriptions of the items inside. Wedding dress. Blue and white china. Christmas decorations. Photographs. Books. Boxes and boxes of books.

Aside from the boxes, the room has many old pieces of furniture—all made of beautiful wood and with a high-level of craftsmanship. Hand-carved dressers, a large armoire, an antique trunk with metal trim, and chairs that pile on top of each other like a trick in a Chinese circus. Framed paintings, like the one I saw in the living room, lean against walls and each other. I look at Margaret and wonder the reason she wants me to see this place.

The wordless woman takes me toward the back where the large armoire looms like a regal queen. A strange feeling descends, like what I felt when I stared down into the Grand Canyon from the edge of a cliff. Cold sweat beads on my forehead and my hands feel numb as if plunged in ice water. I know without being told what is behind the closed doors.

"Who did this to you?" I whisper, the words like bile in my mouth.

Suddenly I hear the front door open, the noise amplifying from the ceiling as if I was standing inside a cave. I feel blood draining from my body. The sound of footsteps travel in a straight path through the living room to the dining room and the back door. Then the front door closes. Another set of footsteps. The Tweedles! What are they doing here?

I feel as though I am free falling into a bottomless pit. I'm not supposed to be here. There is no innocent or legal reason for me to be in a locked basement of a client's house.

Dark thoughts race inside my head. There would be consequences to being found. The Tweedles won't pay me. They'll spread the word about my untrustworthiness as a real estate photographer. My career, the one I had worked so hard to cultivate, the one I chose instead of something lucrative and respectable like becoming a doctor, will collapse. What will be the point then of fighting so hard for it, of being shunned by my family?

*Run,* an internal voice says. *Run and never come back. Run and tell no one.*

I step toward the door. The light above switches off. I stifle a scream behind my cupped hands. Margaret's warm hand is around the crook of my elbow. She tugs at it, urging me to follow. I let her lead me until we stop at a spot in the corner where the concrete walls emit the coolness of the earth. She puts an index finger to her lips. I nod. I may not know her intention but I trust her. It is inexplicable and illogical. An instinct.

The sound of yelling comes from above. I feel like I am a mermaid listening to a passing ship from under water. *What are they yelling about?*

My phone dings, the sound echoing against the walls, startling me out of my skin. I frantically pull it out of my pocket. The light shines its bright rectangular face in the darkness. I look at the message. It is from one of the Tweedles.

*Where are you?* The words say. *Were you at the La Jolla cottage today?*

*How do they—?* My stomach sinks when I realize I made a grave mistake. I left the photograph I took of Margaret on the desk in the master bedroom! I wrack my brain for a believable lie, something to throw them off my track.

My thumbs furiously type. *I went there in the morning. I wanted to take another photo of the backyard in better lighting. But there's a big hole there now?*

Another text. *The photos you took are good enough. Your job is done. Come by tomorrow for the check.*

I breath in relief and reply. *Sounds good. I'm at dinner with friends. Talk to you tomorrow.*

I turn off the phone—not wanting any more sounds or light to give me away—and shove it back into my jeans pocket.

The old woman pulls me further into the basement and settles behind forts of boxes. Outside the small window, the sun sets quickly, leaving me with only Margaret and my fingertips as guides. Surrounded by odd shadows as tall as trees, everything feels surreal. It is as if I am inside a dream and that dream is someone else's.

In the dark, my ears become more acute. I can hear the drumming of my heart, the sighing of my breath, the scratching of the death watches between the walls. I am Alice lost inside the rabbit hole.

I was once terrified of it, this darkness. For a long time I could not face it without wanting to scream. There is a psychological treatment called exposure therapy. The logic is that if you expose the patient to their source of anxiety without the intention to cause any danger, over time they will learn to accept the source as benign and cease to see it as a trigger. So I subjected myself to the dark.

It's funny how you can trick the mind into thinking something never happened when in fact it did. And after a while, you can almost pretend it happened to someone else who you only know a little. But every so often the fear resurfaces—when I am with a man, his weight on top of me, his breathing in my ear. It's horrible for intimacy. I am broken.

What helps is to think of my body not as mine, but as a temporary vessel I'm merely borrowing. I tell myself the crime did not happen to me, my soul, but to this impermanent meat suit that one day will rot in the ground. As will that of the man who trespassed me.

More footsteps come from above, followed by a muffled conversation. In my head I am praying to all the gods whose names I know—for the Tweedles to leave, for me to make it out safely, for Margaret to be at peace. Finally, their footsteps lead to the back of the house. I hear the backdoor slide open. Why are they not leaving through the front, I wonder?

Five minutes pass. I take a step, but Margaret pulls me back. The door to the basement unlocks and opens. My breath catches in my throat and I bring a hand to my mouth to muffle it. The light switches on, hurting my eyes, followed by the sound of heavy footsteps treading down the stairs. Through the gap between the stacked boxes, I see them. First, their shiny black leather shoes. Then the bottom of their crisply ironed pants. Their suit jackets. Their tasteful ties. Their perfectly gelled hair.

I turn to look at Margaret and see revulsion in her eyes—a deep hatred. I realize then the two men were her murderers. I have never liked them but I did not think, with their clean-cut professionalism, they were capable of such a heinous crime.

Then I remember something a philosophy professor once said.

"When you see atrocities and unfairness in the world, first ask, who profits?"

The Tweedles stand to make a lot of money from the sale of this house. Margaret's house. What other ugliness hides behind their manicured façade? Is there even an owner in Connecticut? Many illegal activities are committed within the housing industry. Perhaps this is just one more scheme. Are there other victims like Margaret?

I watch as the Tweedles head toward the armoire.

"Ready?" one asks.

"As ready as I'll ever be. Wish I wasn't wearing my favorite suit though. Can't this wait 'til tomorrow like we planned?"

"It has to be now. I don't know how the girl got a hold of the old woman's photo, or why she insisted she took it."

"Do you think she knows?"

"She can't. I don't think she's all that bright. But if she keeps sniffing around here, she might find out."

"What a nuisance."

"I have a plan for her if she does know. There's plenty of room for a small Asian girl under the pool." They laugh. The high-pitched sound slices me like paper cuts.

They each take off their suit jackets and neatly drape them on one of the boxes. The armoire doors open. I see plastic, layers and layers of it, making the inside look like an opaque pond. One of the Tweedles heaves and the other catches as the weight drops on him. Margaret, fragile and lifeless, neatly wrapped like a cocoon inside a semi-translucent shell, lays in his arms.

I feel my eyes bugging out of my sockets. I have never seen a dead body before, let alone one whose spirit is standing beside me. My arms find their way around her body. Her sorrow transfers to me, striking me like a tsunami. I want to scream, to empty my rage into the room, the world. But all I can do is watch from my powerless corner of the basement.

One of the men picks up the dead Margaret's legs while the other holds her under the arms. Teetering in coordinated steps, they drag her inch by inch through the basement, past boxes containing her life's memories and precious keepsakes. The rustling sound of thick plastic fills the air, scraping at my eardrums and conscience.

*It's your own damn fault you're here.*

*A smart girl wouldn't be in this situation.*

*If only you had minded your own business.*

I feel like dying. Stuck in this unjust moment, I am weak, small. I want to crumble like dry flowers into nothing. Then I hear another voice. It is not mine this time, but Margaret's.

"The world is a tangle of ideas and distrust," her voice says. "A scientist wants what can be proven. A religious man follows the words of his god. An intellect looks for logic. A mystic reaches out with his feelings. A novelist hides truths in lies."

*A photographer believes what she sees behind the lens. Just as a blind man will never see.*

Everyone understands the world from the context of themselves. Not every fact will be believed, not every justice will be served, but the truth still matters. I know what I must do—the only thing I can do. I pull my phone out and turn it back on. Pointing the lens at the two men as they drag Margaret across the floor, I push record. I do not know what will come of it or whether anyone will believe my story. I'm sure some will question it. They may say the video is a hoax or a set-up. Some may doubt whether a person of my profession is trustworthy, just as the Tweedles did. Others may wonder whether the words of a woman are reliable, as they had doubted mine. The fact is, I don't even know whether I'll live through the night. But behind the camera lens is where I see the truth. And it matters.

Whether it is from fear or adrenaline, my mind is oddly clear. It is as if my neurons are overactive, knitting new connections. Things take on different meanings—those I have never thought of. Have you ever heard the sound of a body being hauled up a step? Somehow it reminds me of a Christmas tree being unloaded from the back of a truck. Both heavy with death.

When the hems of the Tweedles' pants disappear out of view, I take a shaky step forward. My legs feel weak under me, as if I am a toddler with marginal control of my limbs. Margaret does not stop me this time and so I take another step, then another, until the night air touches my skin.

The heat of the day gives way to the cold ocean breeze blowing in from the vast Pacific. After the mustiness of the basement, I welcome it, filling my lungs with the sweetness of the night jasmine from somewhere nearby.

I dial the three digits I wished all my life to never use. It rings and I feel both safe and in danger at the same time. I suck in another deep breath and walk toward the side gate, to freedom.

Suddenly the night is darker, ominous. I realize it is not the sky but a shadow. It belongs to one of the Tweedles. My hand loses all feelings. I hear the soft thud of my phone hitting the ground. I scream. A hard fist sinks into my stomach, knocking the wind out of me. Spots pock my vision. My body collapses like a marionette doll with strings cut off. A grip crushes against the bones of my upper arms and my entire body lifts up. My hair whips against my face. Through it, I see glimpses of the earth and the cottage as if they were one.

"Look what I found!" he says.

My feet touch the ground again, but the vice-like grip is still there, crushing my arms.

"Why are you here?" the other asks, his voice demanding.

"The woman." My voice sounds croaky, as if belonging to someone else, as if I've been trekking through the desert. "Margaret wants me here."

I feel a hard palm against my cheek. The iron bitterness of blood fills my mouth.

"Stop lying! Tell the truth. Who sent you?"

Anger wells inside. I spit, my blood landing on a pant leg and leather shoe. The red blooms like a flower. The act of dirtying something of his makes me feel braver.

"I'm telling the truth. And I have evidence. You'll be in jail forever."

"You don't have any proof."

"I saw what you did. I recorded everything."

"Tell us where you put it!"

"Up in the Cloud. Away from your reach," I say, no longer feeling small.

A fist in my stomach. Another between my left eye and cheekbone. My body is tossed up and I fall through the air, like a bird with broken wings. I land on something solid but rubber-like. The sweet air I had hoarded inside my lungs expels. I open my eyes. The left side of my face throbs and burns.

The dead Margaret is under me, still trapped inside layers of plastic.

Around us are walls of dirt. We are lying in the bottom of the deep hole in the ground. In that moment I know, I am to die here with her as my companion.

I turn my broken body and feel the points of a thousand daggers on my skin. Through one eye, the one not swollen shut, I see the murderers standing at the edge of the pit. Their faces look twisted, misshapen. Is it satisfaction on their faces? Fear? It is difficult to differentiate through my tears. I do not want them to be the last image I see.

I shift my gaze to the night sky and look for Vega, the second brightest star in the northern atmosphere. A boy once told me that before we made love. I wonder where he is—the one who got away. It is true what people say about the moment before you face death. The weight that you have been carrying, all your regrets, even the ones you had forgotten, will be remembered. As I flip through the images of my remorse, I realize Margaret is not one of them. Finding her and her truth is what comforts me, makes me stronger.

I see her now. She is no longer bound inside the suffocating plastic. Standing among the grass, she looks out into the sea, her white hair flying in the wind. In the distance I hear the high-pitch sound of birds. Or is it a ship's horn? It grows louder and louder until it overwhelms everything.

A commotion comes from above. Yelling. Screaming. I can no longer see the Tweedles. But I no longer care. Down here, it is calm.

I feel Margaret's warm hand on my cheek. Her face looks down at me. She smiles and the sky takes on the color of her hair, bright against my eye lids. Someone else is speaking, asking whether I'm okay.

I am fine. I am fine. I am...

# The Bench

New York City, U.S.A., 2026

It starts small, in the manner only an existential crisis could. Like a drop of ink. On a white shirt. Right before an important presentation that will determine your survival in a company. In and of itself, the ink is innocuous. It is just ink being ink, serving its purpose. But on that one particular day, in that one particular moment, with your confidence already shredded, it is a bullet through the heart.

August 3, 2026 is that one particular day. For some, it is still coming. For others, it has already passed. For Ravi, it is happening.

Ravi, late twenties with curiosity in her eyes and a penchant for self-destructive patterns, is sitting on her favorite bench in her favorite park, staring at the sun because she can. Her eyes, no longer bound by the same rules they once were, marvel at the different colors inside the burning star. She used to think they were just reds, yellows, and oranges, but there are also blues, greens, and a hint of violet hiding behind the blaze. She watches as the fire storm morphs and molds, shooting out tentacles of flame into its atmosphere. She has been there before, on the sun, and still goes there whenever she feels like a little pick-me-up. There is nothing comparable to the hair-raising experience of being inside an enraged and powerful entity that could care less about your existence. In it she feels peace. It is her equivalent of the "happy pills" she used to take.

Having had enough, she drops her gaze. Her vision is filled with a white so bright, everything looks blown out like an overexposed photograph. Slowly details return, starting with the outlines of the shapes, then the shadows, then the colors. The path before her radiates green from the summer sun filtering through leaves. Along both sides are benches just like the one she is sitting on—iron and wood, painted in forest green. On the path are people of all ages. A toddler teetering, trying to make use of underdeveloped legs too weak to run. A retired couple feeding peanuts to a group of entitled squirrels. They are not supposed to do that, but the squirrels do not know any better. A hot dog man looks at the couple while longing for his wife whom he had to leave behind in the small village of his birth. A runner passes by, her face red from exertion and heat.

Then Ravi sees him. A man sits across from her, like a mirror image, staring at her with growing curiosity. She does not remember seeing him there just a minute ago. He is wearing a dark wool coat with a matching pair of pants and a homburg hat. In his hand is a cane—a decoration. He appears to be the same age as she. And handsome.

Even though wearing a three-piece suit in the sweltering heat of a New York City summer, in and of itself, the man is not an anomaly. She passes those like him, the wearers of antiquated clothing, many times a day. But what Ravi finds most peculiar about him is his face. He wears an expression of unfolding shock—one she has not seen in her kind.

He rearranges his face as best he can and gets up. Instead of disappearing, he walks toward her with the cane leading him, pockmarking the dirt path. Ravi's breath catches. It is a silly thing to do since her lungs no longer need air, but human habits are impossible to shake. She wants to get up, to walk towards the man and meet him in the middle like diplomats from neighboring countries. But it is too late. He is almost here. She sits straighter. It is the only thing she can do.

He lifts his hat once he reaches her.

"Hello," he says, "My name is Joe. Can you please tell me where we are?"

For a second, she wonders whether he is trying to be funny. But his earnest face says otherwise.

"Central Park in New York City," she says.

"I thought it looked familiar, but one can never be too sure."

He casts his eyes on the path then back at her. "I've never seen you here before. Do you come here often?"

She feels her lips spreading into a smile. "I usually come here every day. I've never seen you before either. It's a big park, I suppose."

"You must love this place."

She nods. When you love a place or a person, you always find yourself gravitating toward it. It is true of anyone—living or dead.

"May I?" he asks, eyeing the spot next to her.

She scoots over to make room for him. He sits down, his weight rocking the bench backward. Its age-bent legs make a crunching sound against the gravel underneath. He must be very old. The older a spirit is, the more they can affect the physical realm.

"It's most strange," he says, in a slow and tentative way, "I don't even remember getting here. I was in Scotland, walking the Highlands you see. It was gray and rainy. Then the next thing I knew, I was sitting on a bench in the middle of Central Park in the summer."

He sounds truly mystified. Ravi is pleased to know she did not misconstrue his expression earlier. It is difficult sometimes for her to gauge the feelings of other spirits since she does not spend a lot of time with them. Usually dead people give each other a wide berth. The world is vast and wondrous, and they see no reason to intrude on each other's space. The dead, unlike the living, do not care about country lines or immigration laws. The only thing they care about is peace.

She looks at his pale face and feels pity. It takes a lot to unnerve a spirit. Except for immediately after her death, Ravi does not remember feeling unmoored in her afterlife even if it did not come with instructions. She wants to hold his hand, and so she does. He smiles gratefully.

"When are we?" he asks.

"2026. August Third." She saw the date on the watch of the runner who passed by earlier.

"2026," he mumbles to himself as if it is a formula to a mathematical problem he has been trying to solve.

"Are you okay?" she asks.

He looks at her, his cheeks coloring pink. "I'm sorry for my rudeness. I didn't even ask your name."

"Ravi."

"Please forgive me my nervous state, Ravi. This has never happened to me before—not knowing how I arrived at a place. It usually takes considerable concentration, as you probably know."

She does. Getting from one place to another takes effort. First you form a thought, then you visualize the place in your mind, and finally imagine yourself there. Unless you are summoned by a medium. But even so, you have the choice of answering the call or ignoring it. It is a failsafe (or supposed to be), so you do not accidentally end up at a place you do not mean to be.

"I'm sorry I can't help. It's never happened to me," Ravi says.

She wonders if she should worry. The question of how Joe arrived hangs in the air like wet laundry waiting to dry. But another question surfaces. *Why?*

She has not asked that in a long time. Since being dead, she has assumed that things will be different. So when they are, in fact, different, it is a meeting of expectation rather than a befuddlement.

"Can you recall your day?" she asks, then realizes it is a silly question. Is a day made up of consecutive twenty-four hours or from sun-up to sun-up? And how does it work with the occasional travels back to the past?

Joe taps an index finger against the head of his cane. His lips jut out in thought.

"Well, as I mentioned before, I was in the Scottish Highlands. Just walking. The ground was soggy from a recent rain. It was in the spring.

The year, I could not tell you."

"And before that?"

"A rainforest in Borneo."

"Let me guess, you were also just walking?"

"Yes."

"Hmm…I wonder if that has anything to do with you accidentally showing up here."

"The walking? But I've been doing that for a century. I cannot see it being related."

"Maybe it's the combination of the rainforest and the Highlands."

"Are you suggesting I have triggered some kind of a location-time slip?"

Ravi shrugs. She really does not know. "Maybe it's just one of those things that happens."

"Perhaps it's just an anomaly. We should put it out of our minds. Please forgive me for bothering you."

Joe moves to get up. Ravi does not want him to leave. She likes him, she decides.

"Maybe we should test the theory," she says.

"Test the theory?"

"We'd first go to Borneo. The same place you went. Then after that, the Highlands. Maybe you stumbled on some kind of wormhole for spirits. It'd be a nice discovery, no?"

A skeptical look crosses Joe's face and Ravi feels the familiar gloom of rejection. He must have seen it written all over her for his expression becomes gentle.

"Actually, that's not a bad idea. It can't hurt to test it. We have all this time after all," he says.

He drapes his arm around her shoulders and Ravi feels her heart, her imaginary heart, expanding inside her imaginary chest. He closes his eyes. She follows. She channels the images in his mind, the ones he allows her to see. It is a verdant scene—a thick wall of woven leaves, a jade river snaking in between trees, lacey ferns carpeting the forest floor. She braces herself for the pull—that odd sensation at her center like an invisible umbilical cord being yanked. But it never comes. She opens her eyes and sees the same path in Central Park. Under her is her favorite bench. Next to her is Joe. His eyes are still closed, his face contorting in an expression at once pained and comical.

"We're still here," she says.

He opens his eyes. They have this blank look, as though he could not see her, as if she was not here.

"Maybe I have to do it by myself," he says, almost to himself.

She scoots away to give him space and watches as he repeats the effort of channeling a passage to the rainforest. He looks so serious that she could feel the strength of his concentration vibrating off his skin. She studies his features. Dark eyebrows. A strong jawline. High cheekbones. A straight and thin nose. He has the look she had found so irresistible in men while she was alive.

He opens his eyes. In them is uncertainty. And behind that is fear.

"I don't understand," he murmurs.

"Let me try," she says and closes her eyes.

There is a picture she has in her mind—the one she uses without fail. A red volatile scorching ball of gas. The dancing marbled surface. The explosive solar flares. An angry god. She waits for the pull. Again, it does not come. She opens her eyes and feels the beginning of panic.

"What's going on?" she asks in a whisper.

Joe moves closer. This time, it is he who holds her hand.

"It appears we're stuck," he says.

"Here? Is it this place? Is it just us?"

"We need to find someone else to ask."

Ravi looks around for another dead person, but all she sees are living humans, walking around, eating, and reading, books in hand, as if everything is just as it should be. Then without warning, just as Joe had materialized, another spirit with the same perplexed expression appears on the bench across from them. It is a woman this time. Her skin is wrinkly, the way it was when she had died. Her hair is as bright red as the sun.

The old woman whips her head from side to side, trying to assess her new surroundings. Ravi is reminded of the old Road Runner cartoon. Beep! Beep! Gone. But the woman is still there, transfixed on the bench as if nailed to it. She stares at them both with intensity. Ravi can see the pressure building inside the woman—her eyes growing until they fully stretch; lips parting, little by little, until they make an 'O' shape; her eyebrows raising toward her hairline until her wrinkles rearrange on her face. Pop!

"What the hell is going on?!" the woman yells. "How did I get here?"

She rises off the bench and advances toward them. She is short in stature and hobbles a little as if she had been sitting too long in one spot. But there is no mistaking her air of danger. She looks to Ravi like a vicious and aggravated rabbit—one who could tear her jagged teeth into a lion's neck and eat him. Joe stands up and takes a step forward. The woman stops.

"Did you do this?!" she asks. She wants an answer. And fast.

"Of course not!" says Joe. "The same thing happened to me."

"And who the hell are you?"

"My name is Joe. And may I have your name?"

"Cassandra. When is this?"

"August 3, 2026," says Ravi.

"That's now. At least," the woman says. "Why am I in Central Park? I was just at home."

Joe shakes his head. "We're not sure how this happened. Ravi is the only one who chose to be here. She was already here when I arrived."

He gestures toward the bench. "Would you care to join us?"

Cassandra nods. Ravi scoots over and the old woman sits next to her. Joe takes a spot on the other side of Ravi.

"You said you were at your house. Where is it?" Ravi asks.

"West Fifty-forth and Eleventh."

"That's quite a ways."

"It sure as hell is an inconvenience. I was in the middle of something."

"What were you doing?" Joe asks.

Cassandra looks as if Joe had asked her for her first born child.

"I'm sorry for my intrusion. We were just trying to figure out how I got here. And we thought maybe it has something to do with what I was doing."

"And what was that?"

"Walking. I was in the Scottish Highlands. Before that, Borneo rainforest."

Cassandra looks appeased.

"I was in a book," she says.

Being in a book is one of the spirit world's greatest pleasures. It is nothing like reading. Nor is it like watching a movie. It is living the story as if you are hovering over the shoulder of the storyteller—seeing it, smelling it, hearing it, experiencing it with complete submersion. Naturally, the stories most enjoyed by the spirits are those rich in descriptions and with a strong sense of place. Sadly, most contemporary books are written for the masses whose attention spans are short. They want fast paced plots that zoom along at the speed of light. Although some spirits do not mind the whiplash feel of those books, most prefer the classics. That is the reason libraries are crowded with spirits and ghosts.

"So what have you found out so far?" Cassandra asks.

Ravi and Joe exchange a look—the uncomfortable, awkward look of people who know something bad but do not want to share.

"What? Spit it out if you have anything," the red-head demands. She is as fiery as her hair.

"We can't leave this place," Joes says in a somber voice.

"What do you mean, you can't leave."

"He means we can't leave this park. We both tried," Ravi says.

Cassandra looks skeptical. Then she closes her eyes. The folds of concentration gather between her brows. Ravi prays the woman will disappear. A long minute passes, but Cassandra has not moved.

The woman's eyelids flutter open. When she sees Joe and Ravi, she looks as though she has been poked with a hot stick.

"It's broken," Cassandra says with an inflection at the end, half questioning.

"Yeah, we kinda noticed," says Ravi.

"In all my born days..." Joe says.

Something is wrong, that much is obvious. Still a question lingers. *Why?*

\* \* \*

When Ravi was eight, she came to this park daily with an au pair from Thailand. They lived a few blocks away, in one of the expensive high-rises—both her parents were lawyers. She hated her au pair because the woman only spoke to her in Thai despite knowing that Ravi could not understand. But really, she hated her because whenever the au pair was around, her parents were not, which was most of the day, every day.

One day, in the middle of a summer much like this one, Ravi ran away. She only wanted to scare the au pair a little, but by the time she stopped running, she was lost. Knowing she was the only one to blame for putting herself in this predicament, she was determined not to be scared.

She tried to retrace her steps back to the playground. She walked along the winding path under the canopy of trees, passing grassy fields, boulders and knolls. But soon the trees were beginning to look the same, and so were the green benches and the lamp posts. Slowly the sounds of traffic from Fifth Avenue, as familiar to her as a lullaby, became thinner. She remembered her mom telling her that the closer you are to the middle of the park, the quieter it gets. She began to panic, but she kept walking.

When she came to a fork in the road that split into three, she stopped. Here, the trees were bigger and the ground along the path was thick with shrubs. Ravi was a lover of fairytales and she was reminded of

Little Red Riding Hood. The trees under which she had felt safe just moments ago began to take on an aggressive appearance. Their black trunks and gnarled arms looked as if they wanted to reach out and choke her little neck. A sense of doom crowded out light and she found herself on the verge of screaming. Then she saw it. A bench. She ran to it as if it was a life raft. As soon as she sat down, her anxiety subsided. On this bench, she was protected. On this bench, she was safe.

A policeman found her and she was reunited with the au pair who was waiting in panic at the playground. Neither Ravi nor the au pair told her parents. It became a secret they shared. The au pair left a year after, but Ravi would never forget her.

* * *

"Maybe we should look for more of us," suggested Joe.

"Where?" Ravi asks.

"I'm not sure. Perhaps if we walk to the street, there'll be more."

Ravi knew the danger of walking when lost. The best thing is to stay put.

"I think we should just sit here and wait. Maybe more will arrive. I mean, both of you came to that bench." Ravi points to the culprit across the way. "Maybe it's some kind of portal."

"I'm not into science fiction, but I'll go with it," Cassandra says and settles into her seat.

They all stare at the bench across from them and hold their breath in anticipation of another mysterious arrival. Nothing happens. The bench is still empty. It is just like the moment you call someone to fix your computer only to find that when the person arrives, nothing is wrong.

Cassandra begins to fidget. First, she fiddles with the bow on her blouse, untying and retying it. Then she undoes her curly red hair and regathers it into a bun. Ravi watches with mild interest. The old woman does not seem to like having nothing to do. Then Ravi sees it. A small shape, like a birth mark, sitting just above Cassandra's right temple. It looks like an ink drop—perfectly round with a corona of starburst edges. The strawberry red color stands out against the woman's pale skin, glowing, calling, throbbing like a tiny beating heart. Ravi knows the color. She knows it well.

The old woman notices her stare.

"What?" she asks, her voice annoyed. "Why are you looking at me like that?"

"Nothing." Ravi says and turns away.

Cassandra narrows her eyes. She has been reading people ever since she could talk. She saw the young woman pulling at the edges of her long sleeves with her fingers; the rapid blinking; the subtle wrapping of her arms around her body. She knows Ravi is hiding something up her sleeves and it may be the reason they are stuck together like rats on a bench in the middle of Central Park.

"So what's your story?" Cassandra asks.

No one answers. Joe and Ravi both know by instinct the question is not as innocuous as it sounds. The underlying curiosity is always, "How did you die?" And that is just too personal of a question to ask on a first meeting.

"Don't all share at once," the old woman says. "Alright, I'll go first. If we have to sit here all day, we may as well get to know each other."

Cassandra takes in a deep breath. "I was a sometime-psychic, sometime-medium. The best on the West Side. People travelled from all over the place to see me. There were celebrities too. My most famous client was a Broadway actress of a long running show. You wouldn't know from her performance on stage that she had debilitating anxiety. The only way she could cope was to see me. Once a week. Every week. Until the day I died. Sometimes I wonder if she's alright. But I haven't visited."

Cassandra continues. "That's when my ability disappeared—after I died. I can still talk to ghosts and spirits of course, but so can all dead people. There's nothing special about it anymore."

"And your psychic ability?" Ravi asks.

"No one dead cares to know how their future will pan out. There's no life. No reason to know what will happen. But I'm glad. It was a burden anyway."

"You didn't like knowing?" Joe asks.

"I've never known a life as peaceful as this one. Ironic, isn't it?"

The old woman sighs. "So, now that I've shared my story, I believe the polite thing to do here is to share yours."

Joe clears his throat. "I'm afraid my story is not as fascinating as yours. I was born in Iowa, then I moved here for college on a scholarship and never left. Well, until I died. That's when I began to do all my traveling."

"When did you move to the city?" asks Cassandra.

"It was 1919. I was eighteen."

"What was the city like back then?" Ravi asks.

"Ceaseless with people. Horse carriages and automobiles shared the road. Stalls littered the walkways at all hours. Fresh immigrants arrived daily. Everyone was competing for the space to live and the air to breath. I was used to a quiet life in the country. So I would come to the park a lot. I would find the quietest spot, like this one, to sit among the trees. Just for the silence."

"New York must have looked so different from where you came from," says Ravi.

"I remember the first time I saw the Woolworth building. At fifty-seven floors, it was the tallest building at the time—the biggest thing I had ever laid eyes on."

He felt as if he was in the presence of a Greek Titan. It loomed over the city, readying to smite everyone who passed it.

"What did you study?" Ravi asks.

"Mathematics and economics."

"Useful things to know," says Cassandra.

"Not so much anymore."

"You don't sound like you liked it."

"I only chose the majors at my father's behest. He used to tell me all the time 'You're too smart to be a farmer, Joe.' He didn't want me toiling in a field that belonged to someone else like he did."

"And what did you do?"

"I was a stock broker."

Joe hated his job with every ounce of his being. He remembers thinking ironically that he was leading the exact life his dad did not want him to have—toiling in someone else's field.

"Any living relatives?" Cassandra asks.

"No one in the city. I never married so I only have distant relatives scattered all across America."

"Never found the right girl?" the old woman asks.

Joe's face colors. "I'm afraid I was too preoccupied with my work to have had the pleasure."

"And now?" Cassandra asks.

The red on his face deepens. "To be honest, aside from the two of you, I haven't spoken to anyone else in ages. I'm often by myself."

"The walks..." says Ravi.

Joe smiles. "Like I said, my life is not very interesting."

"And what's your story, girl?" asks Cassandra.

"Umm...I'm not that interesting either. I grew up a few blocks from here, so I come to this park every day."

"A rich girl," says the old woman.

"It's not me. My parents are lawyers."

"They're still alive?"

Ravi nods.

"So you're like, a baby ghost?" says Cassandra.

"I'm not completely new. It's been a few months."

Ravi can feel the woman's stare on her, digging, trying to unearth something else—something precious.

"Why this park every day?"

"I—I just feel safe here. On this bench."

"So you come here every single day to sit on this particular bench when you can be doing anything else?"

"I told you I'm not very interesting," Ravi says, wanting the questioning to cease.

"That may be, but the fact that three spirits who prefer their own company to any other ended up on this bench, on this day, unable to leave, is very interesting."

"You think that has something to do with it?" asks Joe.

"At least it's a start. What else do we have in common?"

"We all lived in New York when we were alive," says Joe.

"Yes, but we weren't all here before we were summoned—or whatever you'd call it—to this place. I was already here. You were in Scotland. And you were in your apartment," Ravi says.

"It's not gender nor age," mumbles Joe. "Could it be our relationship to this place?"

"I got lost here once when I was little and this is the bench I was found on."

"I suppose that's the reason you like it here so much," Joe says.

Ravi shrugs. She never reasons why she comes here. She just does. "I love it here."

"I do too," Joe says with a smile. "It's easy to love this place."

"Yeah. Yeah. Everyone in the city has a relationship with this park. Big deal," Cassandra says.

She looked straight at Ravi. "So what were you doing earlier?"

Ravi shifts in her seat. The old woman studies her and realization blooms.

"Fascinating. You've been sitting here a while, haven't you?"

Ravi looks down. She notices her hands are clutching tightly at the ends of her sleeves. She does not know how long she has been doing that. She lets go.

"If your parents live so close and you just died recently, why don't you visit them?" asks Cassandra.

"I didn't know that's a rule."

"It's not, but it just seems logical. Unless they're monsters."

"They're not monsters."

"So you just don't miss them?" Cassandra asks.

"Of course I do."

"Fascinating."

"Stop saying that!"

Cassandra knows the reason Ravi does not visit her parents. It is the same reason she does not check on her clients. Guilt.

"What are you hiding, girl?"

"Excuse me?"

"There's a piece of information you have that you're not telling us."

"I don't know why you're both here. I was just sitting like I usually do. I didn't summon you or make you stay here against your will. I was just sitting here!" Ravi feels her entire body shaking from anger.

"Okay, Cassandra, that's enough," Joe says. He places his arm around Ravi's shoulders protectively.

The old woman smiles with one corner of her lips as she looks at them. A budding romance, she thinks, is the least she could contribute in this ridiculous situation. But still, she needs to know what the girl is holding back. Her gut feeling is telling her it will provide a clue to their quandary. And her gut is never wrong.

The bench across from them is still empty. The people—the living—around them go about their day in bliss, reveling in the warmth of summer, storing its memory in their DNA for the long harsh winter. A little child in pigtails passes by with an ice cream cone. She laps at it rabidly as it melts onto her hand and down her arm. Lovers walk hand in hand, dreaming of quenching their thirst for each other in privacy. Happy dogs trot around, sniffing everything with unrestrained rudeness. Aside from them, everyone else is oblivious to the three glum spirits among them. A good thing. Cassandra does not wish her ability to communicate with ghosts on any one living even though she was more prepared than most for life after death because of it.

In all her years communing with the dead, she had learned a few things. The spirits left on earth, those who have not transcended (to where, she does not know), are here because they are stuck. They told her they can travel between realms and time, and even to places around the universe. Yet somehow, as if by instinct, they all know they are bound. There are lines they cannot cross, and so they roam and become lost souls. They are, each in their own way, unhappy. And unhappiness radiates and transfers. That was the hazard of her old profession.

A question comes to her. What if a powerful entity had decided to condense their boundary and Central Park is now their permanent container? Talk about elevating the definition of being stuck to a new level! The idea frightens her. Mostly because she does not know the reason it is happening.

"What if this is it? This is where we'll stay forever," Cassandra speaks her fear out loud.

Joe feels his throat closing up. That same concern has been festering in the back of his mind ever since he learned he could not leave this place. He is accustomed to and has come to revel in the freedom death affords him. His life—the one before death—was miserable. It was not his, really, but a jumble of decisions made by someone else. His afterlife is the only thing he has that truly belongs to him.

Cassandra could see Joe circling down the drain of anxiety. He is a wanderer. It is written all over him. He has a constant need to move, to be somewhere else, to run away. Even now, as he sits with his arm around Ravi, he is looking for an exit out. And to a wanderer, being stuck is the end. The old woman sees the same fear in Ravi's eyes, which surprises her. The girl admitted she prefers this place to any other. This bench, this park, is her home.

"So when you can get out, where will you go first?" Cassandra asks.

"I was planning on Antarctica after the Highlands. I wanted to go there again before all the ice melted," says Joe.

"And you, girl?"

"The sun."

"The sun?" Cassandra asks, her face scrunching into a prune.

"Have you never been there?" Ravi asks.

"Never been interested."

"I've never been either," says Joe. "But now I actually do want to go."

"Maybe we can go there together?" Ravi says.

She has never thought of traveling there with anyone else. The sun is a sanctuary of sort, but she wants to bring Joe. He smiles in agreement.

"And you, Cassandra? Where do you want to go?" asks Joe.

"Home."

It is Ravi's turn to look incredulous.

"Don't make a face. My house is very nice. I used a decorator and everything."

"It's still yours?"

"Well yeah, I paid for it. And my trust is paying for its upkeep."

Ravi laughs.

"What's funny?" Cassandra asks.

"I thought the idea of death is that you don't own anything," Ravi says.

"It's comfortable. I know where everything is. It's a good set-up."

"And you made fun of me for liking this bench."

"I did not! I never said a thing."

"Your tone did."

Cassandra rolls her eyes.

"So how many clients did you have besides the famous Broadway actress?" asks Ravi.

"Many. I made a good living."

"You never married?"

"You can't marry with that life. Being woken up in the middle of the night by distraught ghosts looking to talk to their family members does not a healthy marriage make. My clients are my family."

"Oh."

"What?"

"I got the impression earlier that you hated your job," says Ravi.

"I said it was a burden. I never said I hated it. The best thing was being able to help my clients find some kind of peace. It's hard to come by, you know, living in this city. In this world."

"I suppose that's the reason everyone comes here," Joe says as he looks at the changing faces of the living, moseying around in their small corner of serenity.

In the last ten years he witnessed peace, like the ice cap in Antarctica, dwindling. Despite the advances in technology, humanity has not moved forward. Draughts, famine, territorial disputes, genocides, and economic upheaval turned countries against each other. More and more engaged in warfare with an ever fiercer destructive firepower. The world is constantly on the verge of collapsing. To cope, everyone constructs walls around themselves—making tiny islands of tranquility to stand on.

"So how did you help your clients?" Ravi asks.

"Well, everyone came to me because nothing else helped them. Not expensive psychiatrists nor lawyers; nor marriages nor children. Sometimes answers are found in-between places, existing in the gap between logic and reason. I helped women talk to their dead mothers, make peace with their past, clean their aura of darkness. But they helped me too. They made me realize my purpose."

"I wish I had known about you when I was alive."

Cassandra reaches up and touches Ravi's cheek gently, the way she did to her clients. "I would have taken your calls."

Ravi looks down at her hands as she contemplates a decision.

"There's something else we may have in common, Cassandra," she says, finally.

She locks eyes with the old woman for strength and slowly pulls up her sleeves. When Cassandra sees it, she knows what the young woman has been hiding.

In the middle of Ravi's thin forearms are two long parallel lines in bright scarlet. The same color as the mark on Cassandra's temple.

The old woman moves her hand to the spot, then tugs a strand of hair behind her ear to expose it for the two to see.

Joe gasps. Both Ravi and Cassandra look at him. The initial surprise on his face transforms as the meaning unfurls. His hands travel to the top of his white shirt. He slowly unbuttons it. A thick line, as bright red as the marks on Cassandra and Ravi, emblazons his neck.

"Is this our punishment?" Ravi asks in a weak voice.

"Rubbish," says Cassandra. "Why would it take so long if that was the case? Joe's been dead for how long—a hundred years?"

Joe nods. "It's a commonality. But it's not necessarily the reason we are here."

"So why are we here?" Ravi asks.

"Aside from having a giant man with a beard peer through clouds and yell the answer, all we can do is guess," says Cassandra. "But at least we have one clue. A similarity. A reason we share this existence at least."

"So where's everyone else?" asks Ravi.

As if on cue, a tremor begins—like an earthquake, but from deep in her core. A frightfulness unlike anything Ravi had ever felt before grows until it possesses her entire body. She grabs Joe's and Cassandra's hands for anchor and comfort and finds them ready. She has never been so glad to have another's presence next to her.

The bench in front of them is no longer empty. It is filled from one end to the other with dead people whose expressions range from surprise to sheer terror. And not just that particular bench. Up and down the path, spirits occupy every bench for as far as Ravi's eyes can see. Then they begin to appear on the path and in the trees—even inhabiting the spaces of the living, standing in them and around them, like an infestation, covering every inch of Central Park.

Ravi can see in the faces of the living that they are beginning to feel something is amiss. A part of them—the ancient part that senses without apparent logic—sends prickles to the back of their necks and shivers through their skin. They stand frozen, looking at each other with confusion. Everyone, both living and dead, know they are in imminent peril, but nobody knows why.

Faster than anyone can scream, the sky lights up. Ravi watches as the benches, the trees, the lake, the high-rises, the bridges, and the living evaporate into shadows. Angry flame slithers and winds, incinerating all things physical, transforming the surface of the earth into that of a star. The heat in the air dances as balls of fire engulf and destroy. Sounds of explosions and the dead shrieking echo through the emptiness.

Ravi, Joe, and Cassandra look on in horror. Reds, oranges, and bright yellows fill their vision. It is like standing on the sun or being inside an erupting volcano. Had they had skin, it would have melted and turned to dust. Had they had hair, it would have singed off their heads, filling the air with the scent of burning bones. Had their hearts existed, they would have exploded inside their chests. But as spirits, they appear as they did on the day they died.

In the aftermath of the destruction, surrounded by smoldering fields, Ravi turns her head left to right and finds that Joe and Cassandra are still there. Their hands are still holding hers. She is thankful for them. Had they shown up at the same time as everyone else, she would have been facing this chaos alone. The three scan the terrified faces around them and realize their purpose. Without words, they begin their walk through the path of spirits, consoling the lost souls as they pass. No one should feel alone at the end.

# Jasmine Water

Shoulders hunched, Cinta walked barefooted, a red clay jar nestled in the curve of her waist. The hem of her sarong made a swishing sound against her calves. She was tall for sixteen. Taller than even some men.

The grass had been weeping overnight, tormented as if the dark had unleashed a well of painful secrets. Her feet squished into the wet earth, marking it as territory. The croaking of frogs and chirping of crickets paused as she passed, only to resume again.

A wintry wind swept through, and the bamboos around her swayed side to side like long-legged tree spirits dancing to wordless music. From somewhere in the distance a rooster crowed. The sky was changing. The pale light at the horizon lengthened its arms and caressed the indigo above, transforming it into an ombré palette of blues and yellows. Soon everyone in the neighborhood of Kampong Java would rise with the dawn.

Ahead in the haze of a pearly fog, a wooden dock stood lonely on a mound of land formed by generations of silt and petrified hyacinth. It was an image both ethereal and earthly, like the land of the fairies going in and out of view. Here—decades before the creeks were buried alive under freeways and the citrus groves were sacrificed for high rises—was a doorway. Made of translucent things, it was of both worlds. Cinta did not know it yet, but she would be one of the rare

146

few to ever pass its threshold.

A rickety bamboo bridge over a creek connected the dirt path to the dock. It rose and fell with each of her steps. Her mother often told her to be more like the bamboo. Bendable. Affable. Useful. But the girl was more like the wood of the dock. At once unyielding and brittle. In danger of falling apart.

She stepped onto the dock and it teetered slightly under her weight, the wood pulpy and springy from years of submersion in the creek. It was fragile and flawed—impermanent. But that was how things were supposed to be.

Cinta descended the stairs to the river, settling on her favorite step and setting the jar next to her. Down below, through the gap between her dangling mud-stained feet, were eyes. Round, tiny, unblinking—staring up from the water. *River shrimp.* These would be her breakfast for the day.

She gathered the end of her sarong and eased into the cool water. Goose pimples peppered her skin. She bit her bottom lip to keep from shivering and continued sinking into the water, letting it envelop her. Above, the sky shifted ever so slightly as if someone was adding pigment bit by bit as one would a watercolor painting.

She breathed deeply, chasing away the night-staled air in her lungs. The water eased by in no hurry as it journeyed toward the tea-colored Chao Phraya—the vital artery across Siam, connecting it to British Burma in the north and the Gulf in the south. She laid back, floating in the cradle of the water. If she let it, she wondered, would the stream be strong enough to take her all the way to the ocean as it did the fishermen's boats. What would it look like there?

From the corner of her eye, she saw something white struggling in the water like a ghostly fish flitting in a tangle of weeds. She swam forward, closing the gap between her and it. The pale thing was a *malai*, a garland of jasmine flowers Buddhists use in worship. It was half-submerged, a drowning man, in the shallows near the bank where rocks and a raft of water plants gathered.

She plucked the soggy garland from its impending demise—water dripping off it like tears. It was missing flowers in places. Those left were bruised and battered, the tips a shade of caramelized onion. She lifted it to her nose and found the scent still sweet. She wondered where it was from.

Then she remembered. Up the river next to a massive ficus tree was a spirit house. In it lived a ghost, a mother who had lost a child to stillbirth. Cinta was told the nameless woman would wander the riverbank every night, mourning for her dead baby. Perhaps this jasmine garland belonged to her, Cinta thought. Like the spirit house. Like the child.

The smell of burning wood touched her nose, reminding her of the reason she was in the water. She looped the garland around her wrist and swam toward the dock. Under it, around the pillars a colony of shrimp gathered, huddling together for comfort.

The water underneath the wood platform was the color of emerald. Enclosed, like a cave, like an underwater grotto from which stories of mermaids emerged. A palace of green.

She began the process of gathering, plucking each shrimp from its home. They squirmed and kicked, fighting to stay behind. With a firm grip on each shrimp, she swam toward the jar on the bottommost stair.

The sound of walking came from above—hard and heavy—each step like the knocking on a roof by a giant. *Thunk. Thunk. Thunk.* Cinta paused. At this early hour, it could only be one of the women in the neighborhood coming to wait for a row boat destined for the market down river. A mischievous smile touched her lips.

The footsteps terminated just above her at the edge of the platform. The wood creaked with the weight of a body, sitting, two hands on either side like roots. Cinta drifted closer, moving silently through the water like a crocodile readying to snap its jaws on prey. She held both shrimp up, weapons in mischief—their claws clambering to break free.

From the ledge, two legs dropped, at once deliberate and hasty. A controlled fall. But instead of being clothed in a crisp sarong with the black and brown pattern of Java, the legs were in pants. Pale khaki. The fabric was too thick to be practical for Southeast Asia. On the feet were not sandals, nor were they bare, but instead encased in dark brown laced leather boots that went up almost to the knee. Their tips were encrusted with drying clay and grass.

Cinta's eyebrows scrunched together, like the shutting of curtains, the folding of a fan. This was not the clothing that belonged to the Siamese, the natives of this country. Nor was it of the Javanese, immigrants from the land of a thousand islands, like her and her people. It spoke of distant places; of frozen lakes and unnamed trees; of scents unfamiliar and foul. *Foreign.*

It was not entirely uncommon to see a *farang* in Bangkok in 1904. Since the King had signed a treaty allowing foreigners to trade freely in the kingdom, many had settled here. Down the river in the *Bang Rak* district was a port where ships came and went from the Gulf. Next to it was the Danish East Asiatic Trading Company. And further down was a row of enormous colonial structures belonging to European embassies. *But.* The foreigners were not supposed to be here. This enclave, carved from silts and mud, hidden among citrus groves and mango trees, was supposed to be safe from such intrusion.

Cinta knew about the cruelty of the westerners—colonizers of her parents' homeland for hundreds of years. They were evil. Slavers, usurpers, stealers of resources and dignity. They coveted and they took. It was their way.

She slithered back, as silent as a water nymph, and hid behind one of the piles. From here, she was shielded but the stairs to the river were still in her view. *Why is this farang in Kampong Java?* she wondered. He did not belong here. Their kind did not belong here. Just as she did not belong in their mansions behind walled gardens and borrowed luxury. *We live in different worlds*, she thought. They were only meant to intersect on neutral ground out there in the rest of Siam, the only free country in Southeast Asia. This place, a fragile dock on a small island in her *kampong*, was not neutral. Would never be. She wished him gone.

"Do you?" a voice asked. It sounded like a whisper, an echo of someone familiar. It did not come from above but below. "Do you really wish him gone?"

Cinta gasped. The shrimp in her hands struggled loose, scratching her fingers with their sharp claws.

*Who's that?* she said, but no sound came out of her.

Every single strand of hair on her body stood up like soldiers, readying for battle. She felt a scream building up inside. It started in the hollow of her chest, then it grew bigger, bubbling up her throat. But instead of exploding out as it should, it dissipated like the mist in the sun. It was as if a blanket of calm had been thrown over her, nullifying her fear.

"You don't need to be frightened of me," the voice said.

*Who are you?* Cinta thought.

"I am the water, the wind. A mother whose heart has been shattered into fireflies."

*You can hear my thoughts? Are you inside my head?*

The voice laughed. "The only voice inside your head is you, Cinta. I am simply—listening."

*Why are you here?*

"Why am I here? Why are you here? Why is the boy here? What's the purpose of this meaningless moment in the years that came before and will come after?" A sigh. "Except it's never meaningless, is it?"

*Where did you come from?*

"Everywhere. Nowhere. The future. The past. It's difficult to keep track sometimes."

The voice was making Cinta feel heavy, as if she was under layers of blankets, as if the bones in her limbs were made of stone. She felt like closing her eyes and drifting. She tried to imagine a better place—somewhere safe.

"Stay with me, Cinta," the voice said. "I'm afraid there's no way to escape this moment. At least not yet."

*What do you want with me?*

"We're just going to talk. A conversation. Between you and me."

*About what?*

"The boy for instance. Aren't you the least bit curious about him?"

*No. I do not wish to know him nor his unpleasant people.*

"Ah…there are no innocents in a guilty race, is that it?" The voice paused as if contemplating her. "He's about the same age as you. His name is Adam."

*Why is he here?*

"He's here because he must. Because there's no other place he can be right now. Your fate and his are tied together."

*Why? I don't want him here.*

"That may be. But nevertheless, you and he are connected. At least until—"

*Until what?*

The voice said nothing back.

Cinta could see him now, the boy, Adam. He was sitting with his back to her on the bottom stair—her favorite step. His shoes were no longer on his feet. His pants legs were rolled up to his knees. His skin, pale pink like that of a newborn, glowed in the blue dawn. The hair on them and his head was golden, the color of rice straw. He appeared to be unaware of her presence.

"He can't see nor hear you or me," the voice said.

*Why not?*

"Because I don't want him to. It is you whom I want to speak with. Not him."

The girl felt like crying. She was a prisoner of this disembodied being, whatever it was.

*How do I get out of this?*

"As I said, we just need to talk. Is there something you want to know about Adam?"

Cinta forced her brain to think of more questions. If she had wanted to know the boy, what would she be curious about?

*Where's he from?*

A scene appeared in front of her. It was faded, bleached of colors. The sky above was gray, covered by thick clouds and smoke. A crowded street. Horse-drawn buggies. People walking, wearing strange clothes—the clothes of the foreigners. Everything reeked of horse excrement. The vision disappeared.

*What happened?!*

"You just saw his memory of where he's from. A land faraway."

*How was I able to see it?*

"Nothing's impossible right now. Not here, in this moment."

*I don't understand.*

"Don't worry, Cinta. You will."

*What's he doing here?*

"Remembering. He misses home."

*But this place looks nothing like his home.*

"The place you saw is not where he sees as home. For nine years he lived in *Nan*, a province in the north. He had lived there for longer than he had lived anywhere else. Although he could never call it home."

*Why not?*

"It's not the way he was taught to see things."

*There are other riverbanks, other creeks. Why can't he find some other dock to sit on to reminisce about wherever home is?*

Cinta watched as Adam reached for the clay jar, hers, red-brown, earthy. He picked it up and peered inside its void. He shook it. He blew into the opening and made the sound of a ship horn as it leaves a port.

This time she saw a pier crowded with people. They were wearing the same strange clothing as in the first vision. She saw them as though she were an eagle in an aerie. She was high off the ground, higher than she had ever been. The people were waving. But she was not waving back. There was no one there she knew.

Her hands gripped the rail, her knuckles taut, the skin white and shiny thin. She realized these were not her knuckles, not her hands.

She looked at the clothes on her body—brown pants and jacket made of thick fabric that itched. She was not herself. She was him, and he was a boy saying goodbye to no one.

*Does he not have family?* she asked.

"Only his father."

*Where's his mother?*

Another vision rose. She was in a room, standing next to a bed. A woman lying on it, her hair spreading around her like river weeds, her face pale of color. Cinta felt something hard the size of her fist plugging her chest.

*Where's his father?*

"Searching for peace. A new place to worship in."

*Here?*

Cinta saw a long room. At the end was a cross. She knew of the cross. A man stood in front of it. He was speaking. But the constant ruckus from the outside punctured through the wood walls, rattling the window panes.

The weight inside her chest transformed to anger, fierce and fiery.

*They don't belong here!*

Was there no place safe for her and her people from these colonizers who felt entitled to the world? She wanted to cry at the injustice of it all but the well of her tears was dry, drained by the enforced calmness that cocooned her. She felt like a chrysalis, bound and unborn.

What did she do that made her deserve the cruelty of this moment? Perhaps she was in a dream, a nightmare. Lit by the shimmering green light beneath the dock, the world seemed fantastical and false. It was not difficult to think this a dream.

"It is not," the voice said, reminding Cinta she was still trapped. "I'm sorry, my dear child, but this is real. And you must embrace it."

*Is this your doing? This curse?*

The voice laughed again, the sound as crisp as the tips of snow pea shoots. "I do not possess such power."

Cinta thought of her family. Of her mother sitting in front of a stove, stirring the fire, coaxing it to the perfect temperature for cooking. Of her father's serious face as he counted the oranges they had picked from the grove, readying them for the market. They had not yet begun the process of wondering, of worrying. She missed them.

*I wish to go home.*

"You will."

*When?*

The voice was quiet. Thinking. Cinta wondered what thoughts would enter a mind without a body.

"I, like you, only know what's been revealed," the voice said, finally.

*Then tell me what you know.*

Suddenly, Cinta felt a grip squeezing her organs as though they were clay, molding them into form. She gasped for breath. It came up short and labored. She was drowning. Not in water, but in something heavier and thick. She was an insect trapped in amber.

Colors whirled and spots pocked her vision. Images came in and out of focus. Everything turned bright white, burning her eyes. Then the light muted, transforming into a small warm glow. It swayed to the rhythm of her footsteps. She was holding a lantern. But her hand was of an old woman—the papery skin was wrinkled and marked with brown spots.

A scent of jasmine permeated the air. Burning incense. The smell stirred an unfamiliar feeling inside her—an aching near her heart. A deep sadness. It felt solid, a lead ball, a shackle that weighed her down, grounding her to the wood floor boards under her feet.

"Regret will one day consume you," said the voice. "It will turn you into a dead star, taking everyone who is strung to you in a karmic web down a path of destruction."

Cinta knew of karma—the concept of fate as an effect from the sum of a person's actions throughout their existence. But she could not understand what it had to do with her. It was not her belief.

"We don't simply float around the universe by ourselves, my dear girl. We're connected to others as we travel through life and they are in turn connected to others. The decisions we make today can affect many lives across time and space."

A series of faces appeared in front of Cinta. A girl not much younger than her, her back against a barren landscape. An old man floating in water, his face a pit of desolation. A woman with black tears on her cheeks. A bearded man reading a book in a language she could not understand. A young girl with hair the same color as Adam's. A couple sitting in front of a large and shiny black shape. Every face floating, slipping in and out of view. She was walking in a dark corridor with crumbling bricks. She was scared. Someone was following her. She was in danger.

Something flew against a dark background. Like a bird, but cold, silver, hard. Orange and red balls of light lit up the night. Like the fire of her mother's stove, but bigger, ever growing. Burning her. Then the sky turned bright cerulean and happy. Against it, she saw two glittering forms, tall and proud, standing erect like swords. Another silver bird. An explosion, two. Tiny figures, human-like, were freefalling through the air. Columns of black smoke rose in their place.

Now she was sitting, surrounded by verdant trees. The hardness of a bench dug into her skin. A blast lit up the world, piercing her eyes with its brightness. A sea of orange enveloped her, its edges dancing, melting off skin. She was gone. Cinta's body shook from fear.

*What was that?!*

"A reality," the voice said. "One of the many iterations of it. Everything traces back to this moment. Everything you saw. They all happened because you had made a choice. You're the pebble that started a ripple in a pond. The decision you made—will make—will lead there. Your connections all tried, will try, to make things better. Some will succeed. Some will be stuck, barely able to hang on to life."

Adam was in front of her again. She watched as the jar slipped from his hands and dropped into the water. He reached for it, but it bobbed away, slowly, being carried off by the stream. He grabbed the railing of the stairs, just as he did the railing of the ship, and leaned forward.

His finger almost touched the jar. *So close.*

With a loud crack, the stairs broke off from the dock, unable to support his weight. The boy tumbled into the water. The stairs collapsed over him. The water turned red-brown, thick as blood. The air smelled of iron. The red crept toward her, fingers searching for a place to cling.

Cinta heard her own scream. The sound echoed and bounced in the cave of her mouth, never making it out, lost like a child inside a dark forest. She began to panic. Another wave of calm—the constant whooshing sound of water—washed tranquility through her like a cleansing monsoon rain.

"Open your eyes, child," the voice said.

Cinta did not know they were closed. She shook her head. She did not want to see the dead boy.

"Open your eyes."

The girl slowly lifted her eyelids. Adam was still there on the bottommost stair. He was staring ahead in silence as if praying. Cinta sighed in relief.

*That was another reality?*

"Yes, if you do not take the correct path."

*But what did I do? What must I do?"*

"Choose."

*But what am I choosing? How can I choose when I don't even know the choices before me?*

"I'm sorry I can't answer your questions. They're beyond me. The only thing I know is that it has affected—will affect—more than you think it will. Whatever decision it was, perhaps, if you can make it differently, things will change. Perhaps a better reality will be in its place."

The constraining weightiness lifted from her. Her arms and legs were no longer as heavy as stone. Her body undulated to the flow of the water. The cocoon no longer bound her. She was free.

"Wait!" she yelled out, her voice echoing under the dock.

She blinked to chase away the green haze. When her vision cleared, she saw Adam looking at her, his eyes wide and bewildered. She was exposed, no longer hidden behind a column. Although he was a few arm strokes away, it felt as if they were across a wide chasm. In that moment she realized that while she had seen them in the streets of Bangkok, she had never truly looked into the face of a foreigner before.

She studied his face. It was different than those of her people—sharper, skinnier, lighter—but there were things similar in it too. The color of his eyes was different, but it was just as familiar to her as the sky. The expression in them—perplexed, confused, curious—reflected the way she was feeling. But there was also gentleness behind the blue. They did not look like they belonged to someone who would destroy the world. Her world.

She felt a rush of empathy toward him—the boy who only a moment ago was floating lifeless in the river. She looked for the jar, the culprit in that death, and saw it still in his hand—red-brown, like the bloody river in the vision. She swam toward it and Adam. Her movement startled him and the jar slipped from his hand. She caught it before it hit the river.

One corner of his lips turned up. A smile. He greeted her in the language she knew.

*Here was where stories began.*

# Afterword

*Before the story was the place, and another story.*

They say writers write from experience. While my life is not as fantastical as that of the characters, many of the tales were inspired by the places I've been to and the stories I've heard. Because of them I believe there's magic in the world.

I grew up in a house similar to the one in **SHADOW PLAY**, in an enclave of Indonesian settlers in the middle of Bangkok surrounded by cemeteries. While children in the west grew up on fairytales, I learned parables through ghost stories and mythologies. The character in **THE WITCH DOCTOR** was inspired by one such story, a neighborhood rumor.

At the age of twelve, I immigrated to a town in Southern California, which became an influence for the desert town in **CALL ME BLUE**. The first friend I made in school (who is still my best friend to this day) told me about the little people who lived on the wall of her childhood home, which sparked the idea of the little thumb monsters in **LOVE ME, TENDER**. The hotel in the same story was modeled after the place in San Francisco I lived in one summer following college. After my very cold three months there, I relocated for a year to humid Southeast Asia. The experience of the main character in **DUST BOUND** mirrors how I felt as a young person in the process of defining my identity and the concept of "home".

Then an event that redefined America happened. **GLIMMER GLASS** was my way of telling a "where I was on 9/11" story and an attempt to understand it in the context of history. Living in America was different before and after that day. Everything was suddenly so black and white—boxed in. In **GHOST MOON**, I wanted to explore tragedy-induced fear of an uncertain world in a safer space—the paranormal. The idea of using a medium to foresee and intercept the future came from a dear friend. **THE WOMAN IN THE GARDEN** was my way of exploring social injustice and the length one must go to be seen or heard. The idea of a mysterious woman no one else could see was based on a real story told by friends.

In **THE BENCH**, I imagined humanity's worst fear come true. I couldn't think of a better setting than Central Park, one of my favorite places to be. To bridge all the seemingly disparate tales together is **JASMINE WATER**. A blend of an eastern ghost story and a western fairy tale, it represents my philosophy that all things are interconnected, and decisions, however small, can affect the course of the future.

In the end, it is my hope that we can all write a better reality.